Thi␣

ENDLESS EMPRESS

Mass Murderer's Guide to Dictatorship
in the Fictional Nation of Enkadar

Kirkland Ciccone

Published by
Strident Publishing Ltd
22 Strathwhillan Drive
The Orchard
Hairmyres
East Kilbride
G75 8GT

Tel: +44 (0)1355 220588
info@stridentpublishing.co.uk
www.stridentpublishing.co.uk

Published by Strident Publishing Limited, 2014
Text © Kirkland Ciccone, 2014
Cover art and design © Ida Henrich

ISBN 978-1-905537-72-3

Typeset in Optima by Andrew Forteath | Printed by CPI

ABOUT
KIRKLAND CICCONE
(Supreme Master of Weirdness)

Kirkland Ciccone's debut novel, *Conjuring The Infinite*, won the 2014 Catalyst Book Award. In recognition of this, he awarded himself the title of Supreme Master of Weirdness. (Moto: *'Be at one with the oddness.'*)

Kirkland has rapidly gained a reputation as one of the most entertaining YA/adult crossover authors, and visits festivals, schools and libraries throughout the land.

As well as being the Supreme Master of Weirdness, Kirkland also writes and performs wonky one man shows. His gigs include *The Dead Don't Sue*, *A Secret History of Cumbernauld* and *The A-Z of Kirkland Ciccone*.

You can follow Kirkland on all sorts of social media and websites, including:

www.kirklandciccone.com
www.twitter.com/KirklandCiccone
www.Facebook.com/ConjuringTheCiccone
www.Instagram.com/KirklandCiccone
www.stridentpublishing.co.uk

"AND ON THE FIRST DAY
OF THE REVOLUTION..."

Her Holiness the Endless Empress of Enkadar skipped to school. Her lightness of step betrayed her exhilaration. The hem of her prom dress was splashed black with the dirt from the many puddles dotted along the route. She carried a little tin lunchbox. It was a heavy but encouraging presence, and not only because it fitted snugly between her arm and hip.

The Endless Empress dreamed of many things. She dreamed of burning bodies in the wreckage of her school. She dreamed of revolution and freedom. She dreamed of Enkadar, faraway and yet within touching distance.

She dreamed of these things and more.

And Her Holiness had a way of making her dreams come true.

DEAD TEENAGERS
The Hunt for the Endless Empress

They sat facing each other in the café, separated by suspicion and a shabby plastic table.

The table was covered in a shredded grey tablecloth that might have been black at first. It wasn't an upmarket café – it had failed every major cleanliness check invented by the Department of Health. The last inspection had gone badly after the examiner made a rather grisly discovery in the pantry; a workbench and buzz saw sitting on top of a refrigerator! If customers knew that the owner marinated his sandwich meat in his household bathtub, they would probably smash the place up.

The café hadn't always been so cheap and nasty; it had once been an award-winning chippie back in the sixties. People had come from across the country to get hot chips soaked in vinegar, drenched in salt. Now the cafe was a pink-painted plastic monstrosity filled with cheap furniture and nasty chips from a new (cheaper) supplier.

Molly McCrumb: Kickass Journalist knew all of this and much more. But she said nothing as she stared into the twitchy eyes of the girl seated across from her.

Silence was confidence.

THE MOLLY MCCRUMB FILES –

from a serialisation in the Castlekrankie Chronicle

The email arrived too late for me to read it, so I got it first thing the next morning. But it made me think about the sort of person who would send an email after midnight.

What keeps that sort of person awake at night?

The subject line told me everything I needed to know:

DO YOU STILL BELIEVE IN THE ENDLESS EMPRESS?

Another two emails arrived soon afterwards:

ARE YOU SEEKING HER HOLINESS THE DIVINE ENDLESS EMPRESS OF ENKADAR? CLICK ON THIS EMAIL IF THE ANSWER IS YES!!!

The third and final email didn't have a subject line, but a list of names.

RICHARD, NAIMA, ELIZABETH, TRUMAN, CARLY, PORTIA.

Someone was urgently trying to catch my attention, someone who knew all about The Endless Empress. *I* wanted to know all about The Endless Empress too. So I clicked and read the message. Then I followed the trail to a grubby place called Go Joe's Café.

The strange girl sat in front of me insisted on meeting at the cafe. I agreed, of course, because I desperately needed a source for this story. I would have met this informant on the Moon if she had desired it. Unearthing new insights was crucial if I hoped to sell my story to a newspaper. And even though I needed the cash, this meeting wasn't just about money or prestige. It was about something else, something I've wanted since I left home.

Some dreams are more realistic when left unspoken.

***

"I like this place a lot," the strange girl said in a wistful voice.

"Likewise," Molly lied unashamedly. It was necessary for her to gain trust, and she had no problems lying. She was skilled at faking trustworthiness.

A waitress with trashy peroxide hair and a bad attitude moved towards the table. She offered sandwiches – an offer Molly was ready to accept, until the crazy girl shrieked from the other side of the table,

"Don't eat the sandwiches!"

"But I didn't have anything for breakfast," Molly said somewhat indignantly.

The erratic girl covered her eyes and replied, "The guy in the kitchen has Hepatitis C. I heard him on the phone talking to his doctor about the results last week. Never, ever eat the sandwiches."

Molly froze as the words stretched out into significance.

She turned and faced the waitress, giving a clown smile, but declining her offer.

"You must think I'm crazy," the crazy girl said sheepishly.

Molly didn't know how to reply to that comment, so she decided to be honest.

"The idea crossed my mind," Molly admitted. "I haven't yet uncrossed it."

***

During her time at high school, the crazy girl had been a lieutenant of The Endless Empress. Both were members of a very special club. They changed their names and flirted with fantasy. The Empress created a world into which the others inserted themselves – until it was far too late for them to escape.

***

Molly knew *nearly* everything there was to know about the crazy girl. She had prepared for this interview with scrupulous research. Molly also knew the mad girl's full name: Carly Costello. Carly was in the process of recovering from some sort of undisclosed illness. There were other things about the established story that Molly found confusing. But Carly was a confusing girl. The whole situation was confusing!

For every story Molly heard about The Empress and her friends, there was a story to contradict it. Molly had spent days sifting through all the files, notes, newspapers and blogs relating to The Empress and the murders.

She had no idea what to make of the jigsaw of facts and fiction.

Carly, however, could help Molly write the biggest story of her career. The crazy girl's function in things was significant. She was the only real link Molly had to her prey: the one and only, the supreme, mythological Endless Empress of Enkadar.

Molly would endure Carly's madness if it gave her a chance to discover the truth.

Questions, Molly thought to herself, *so many questions.*

If The Empress is the question then what is the answer?

"I want to talk to The Empress," Molly blurted out. "Where is she hiding?"

But Carly wasn't listening to Molly. She was humming a little tune.

After a few minutes, Molly couldn't take any more. It

was time to shock the girl back into sanity. And Molly knew just what to do. She tackled Carly with a harsh question.

"Did you help The Empress kill everyone at school?"

Good sense returned abruptly. Carly literally changed her tune.

"I'm not a murderer," she said flatly.

"I don't believe you."

"I was put on trial with the others and found NOT GUILTY."

Then Carly stopped and added somewhat mysteriously:

"If The Empress doesn't kill me, then my Conscience might get there first."

Molly remained silent. She didn't know where Carly would take this interview. It would be difficult keeping her fixed on the matter at hand. Molly decided her interview technique had been too aggressive – there were other ways to make an interviewee speak candidly. She had to be charming and personable. Easy!

"I went to the same school as you," Molly confessed, as a way of creating a bond. "Long before The Empress unleashed her Masterpiece."

***

You already know the best bits of this story. You also know the worst bits. It made the front page of every newspaper in the country. And one face accompanied the reports: the face of a thirteen-year-old girl whose eyes were wide and remote. The Endless Empress called it her "masterpiece" – the explosion that killed over a thousand teenagers. The word masterpiece soon became Masterpiece. The atrocity needed a capital letter. The pupils entered Castlekrankie High School at nine o'clock on a Monday morning...but never left. The blast itself only lasted a few seconds, but the aftermath was days of fire and nearly four years of heartache.

Their school became a mass grave.

What happened to the victims wasn't a Masterpiece, it was an obscenity.

***

"Sometimes I feel I've never escaped high school..." Carly said with a grim smile.

At last! Molly thought triumphantly. *She's going to tell me everything.*

But then, as if a gust of wind had blown her thoughts off course Carly said dreamily, "I won't ever eat the sandwiches."

Then, for some reason, she added in a matter of fact voice:

"Sandwiches are funeral food, and The Empress always liked sandwiches."

Molly knew exactly how to get the truth out of the mad girl. Carly had inadvertently given the crafty journalist a way to dig up more information.

"The Empress liked sandwiches when she was alive?" Molly asked innocently.

"*When* she was alive?" Carly laughed, drawing startled expressions from the peroxide waitress and regular customers. "The Empress is *still* alive. I'll tell you everything. I'll tell you what happened to the old gang. If you listen, Molly, I'll talk. I'll tell you all about our world. I'll talk and talk until you have your answer."

Bingo, thought Molly triumphantly. *Now I know for sure the Empress survived the explosion. But where is she? And will she come out of hiding?*

But Molly knew that catching The Empress wouldn't be easy.

It might not be that safe either.

Because Her Holiness made bad things happened to good people.

SEEK AND HIDE

The fractured little town of Castlekrankie is locked into perpetual winter. But it offers consolation prizes for anyone willing to put up with the warped architecture and icy pavements. It has something for everyone, including an award-winning shopping mall, a bingo hall, a gym, a college and a colossal library.

Yes, Castlekrankie has everything you could possibly want and so much more.

It also has a serial killer. Once upon a time, he killed men and women and animals.

But this isn't a silly fairy tale – it actually happened, here in Castlekrankie.

***

The press called him The Bookworm, even though his real name was Ralph Docherty. They gave him this nickname because he enjoyed reading to his victims before throttling them. For two years the mysterious (and literate) killer terrorized the people of Castlekrankie. For two years, no-one knew whether he would be caught or not.

But The Bookworm made a fatal mistake that led to his downfall.

He kidnapped Portia Penelope Pinkerton. On her seventh birthday.

And he let her live.

***

"It's my birthday and I want to play hide and seek!"

Carly was cold and miserable and her feet were wet. Portia's mother bought her the finest welly boots, but Carly had to make do with the same red shoes she wore every day. They were falling to bits and sometimes, when Carly was sitting, she could smell her feet. She was terrified everyone at school knew she couldn't afford new shoes.

Now she was suffering the arctic blast of a Castlekrankie Christmas, and for what? So she could be with her best friend on her birthday. Carly was so hungry she was gasping to taste a bit of Portia's amazing birthday cake. It was white like the snow around her, and it had three tiers...and it looked so good. The cold made Carly's skin tingly and ruby red. It was dreadfully uncomfortable, but Carly endured it regardless.

"I'll count to ten and come and find you!" Portia – snugly wrapped in her little red hood and scarf, which matched the colour of Carly's cheeks – was already counting.

Outrage nearly floored Carly:

"I need more time to hide! You can't just count to ten. Please make it twenty!"

"This is my birthday, my game, and my rules!" Portia said snippily, her arms folded against her chest. "Or you don't get any birthday cake!"

Reluctantly, Carly complied with her best friend's command. But mutinous thoughts briefly flitted inside her head: Portia was *so* immature for a seven-year-old!

Carly waited until she heard the counting start. When this happened, she burst into action. She looked around for somewhere to hide, but not too good a place in case it took too long to be found.

She had an abundance of places to hide, because they were in the middle of an old factory, full of pipes and promise and – in the end – futility.

***

Castlekrankie is divided into sections, cut up just like a birthday cake, or like a dead body on a mortuary slab. There is the main housing area for people to live and love and hate. There's the business and trade area that contains the ghastly shopping mall, the train station and airport... and there is also the industrial estate. Factories were built in that area, and they became the lifeblood of the town; jobs and work and money for everyone. And then it all ended.

Now they're empty places where two little girls play hide and seek.

But little girls aren't the only ones who hide and seek.

***

Carly decided to play a prank on Portia, and run away home. She was sick of being bossed around and humiliated for scraps of lunch and birthday cake. She was tired with always having to be the Princess's ugly sister in their games. Portia, however, would be the beautiful princess in *every* game they played. When they played pop stars, Portia would be the glamorous idol, and Carly would have to ask for autographs. When they played pirates Portia told Carly that girls couldn't be pirates, only boys – and then turned herself into the Pirate Queen, whilst Carly had to make do with being a slave girl.

I'm not playing anymore, Carly thought defiantly as she raced through the snow with wet feet.

***

Portia stopped counting and began her search. She could see her breath swirling into rings and patterns. She stopped moving through the old factory to watch the outlines, temporarily mesmerized by nature's random whimsy.

When she looked up, her eyes fell on an abandoned

metal locker.

"I know where you're hiding, Carly!"

Portia skipped over to the locker and pulled it open, despite the rusted hinges.

It was empty.

"I don't want to play hide and seek anymore. It's boring," Portia squealed.

But no-one answered except a few red robins bobbing along.

"You're not getting any cake if you don't come out here right now!"

A shadow fell across Portia, and she smiled a wide triumphant grin. Carly always came back, even when she was angry.

But Portia quickly realised there was something wrong with the shadow – it wasn't little-girl sized.

Portia looked up, up, up, up to see a skinny man in a boiler suit. He peered down at her, his face blank. His head was the shape of an egg, and Portia could see blotchy brown marks dotted across his scalp. It revolted her.

The man didn't say anything, yet, because he wasn't ready to read the first chapter. Portia knew fine well never to talk to strangers, so she turned away from the new arrival. She stood in cold quietness, waiting. Large hands, man hands, pushed onto her back. Portia screamed, because she hadn't expected him to put his hands on her. She felt the hands shove her forward with ferocious strength.

The momentum carried her all the way into the locker.

Then the locker door slammed shut.

All was dark and gloomy. The smell of stale petrol invaded Portia's nose. She gagged and coughed. Her coughs sounded thunderous in the cramped metal box.

"Chapter One," a quiet voice said in a crisp English accent.

Portia screamed and begged for help.

***

Portia was later found wandering the streets in a daze – a little red dot in the middle of a snowstorm. She seemed alright, but Carly knew she wasn't. Something was different about her best friend; something had taken root inside her. Portia had become dark, just like the inside of the locker.

The newspapers told the world that Portia was BRAVE and HEROIC for surviving her ordeal. According to a police psychiatrist, Portia only survived by retreating into an imaginary world – a realm deep inside her head that The Bookworm couldn't reach.

This place didn't have a name yet.

That would come later.

A few days after Portia's miraculous return – a day or so before The Bookworm hanged himself in his cell because it had become illegal for prisoners to have books sent into prison – Carly saw the cigarette burns on her best friend's arms.

"Did he do that to you?" she asked in a hushed voice.

But Portia didn't answer. Her expression said everything she needed to say.

Carly burst into tears and pushed away her stale slice of birthday cake:

"I didn't know he was watching us. I didn't mean to leave you."

There came no reply.

"I'm sorry," Carly sniffled.

Portia didn't say anything at first, instead smiling benignly.

Then she finally spoke, for the first time in days.

"We're going to play pirates today."

Carly nodded, because she knew she couldn't disagree ever again.

"I'm going to be the pirate queen," Portia said vaguely.

Carly nodded. She perceived an odd sort of darkness in Portia's eyes; a repressed fury, or a spark before a rampaging forest fire.

"Yes," Portia said, distantly. "We're going to play *my* game..."

***

"You've played her games ever since that day," Molly declared.

Carly smiled, but didn't answer back.

THE LUNACY LEGACY

The Hunt for the Endless Empress

It was the hardest thing in the world living a normal life after a school massacre. This was Naima Calmar's main problem, the quandary she had suffered ever since the day of the bomb. Even now, years after the explosion, people blamed her for the bloodbath. But this wasn't her only problem. Naima had many of those and life wasn't getting any easier.

***

Naima was impatient for Kai to return home. He was already late, and that made her nervous. It had taken hours to get the baby to sleep: the terror that she might wake up was as strong as the fear that Kai might go to the pub instead of bringing home his wages.

"But he paid my electricity bill last week," Naima said aloud to her sleeping baby, "so he *must* be in love with me."

She should have been more confident after losing her extra weight – she'd gone on the 'Class A' diet and slimmed down spectacularly as a result. Naima's narcotic of choice was a mysterious gritty powder known simply as gear.

No-one knew where it came from, but the streets were suddenly full of dealers turning a tidy profit. This strange new drug came in a variety of candy-coated colours and each powder had a different effect on the user. Purple made you forget your problems. Green made you so happy you could die from joy – and some users did die. Pink made you friendly and gracious. (Doctors vainly lobbied the government to allow pink gear to be placed into the nation's water supply.) Red gear made you unbelievably brave but foolish. Blue made you leave your body for a few hours.

I've been told blue gear was the most addictive of all.

Gear, also known on the street as 'G', is a miracle substance. But like all hard drugs...it takes a grave toll on the user's health. The first story I filed for this paper was an exposé on the insidious effects of gear. I didn't get the chance to follow this story through. I became obsessed with tracking down the infamous Endless Empress of Enkadar.

I had no idea the two stories were actually connected.

***

Naima's gear addiction quickly became the least of her many problems.

Someone, without any warning, placed a distinctly sinister advert in the local paper. It wasn't so much an advert, more an announcement. It broadcast a special school reunion for the Citizens of Enkadar. Naima wasn't aware of the news until it smacked her on the face. It actually did smack her on the face! Kai had flown into a rage and hit Naima on the face with a rolled-up newspaper. Why? Because Naima bought her boyfriend the wrong brand of cigarettes – what a silly girl! Kai was *always* chastising Naima for her uselessness as a girlfriend. He took colossal pleasure in reading the reunion announcement aloud over and over again.

CITIZENS OF ENKADAR
High School Reunion
NO LUNCHBOXES ALLOWED

It had to be a sick joke! Who would put something that nasty in a newspaper? Besides, Naima was far too happy with her life to attend some weird reunion. She never wanted to see her ex-friends ever again. High school hadn't been that long ago, but it wasn't long enough in Naima's opinion.

Naima looked around her living room, pausing to fix a Venetian blind that had been tangled up after her last time over at the window. Her black leather couch was already peppered with rips and holes. She frowned. She hadn't noticed how bad it looked in the harsh light of the lamp. Her plasma television had a large crack on the screen, a result of a brawl between her and Kai over what they should watch. She had wanted to watch her favourite soap but he had insisted on seeing the big match. They didn't have cable (it had been cut off) so Kai had kicked the television over and roared at Naima until she'd stopped crying.

This was never a problem before I got pregnant, Naima thought remorsefully. But that felt like a long time ago. And yet for one brief burning second…she pined for a lost life. Naima had hated high school. She had loathed the nasty girls with their sharp tongues. She had despised the boys with their wandering hands. But sometimes, in dark moments, Naima missed The Empress and school. It was ironic that her time as a Citizen was the only period of real camaraderie she had ever known. That stupid club had been her whole life.

Then The Empress had opened a lunchbox and sent everyone to hell.

***

The so-called Citizens of Enkadar turned on each other and the fallout was catastrophic. There is no virtue in pretending to be part of a greater cause when so many innocent people are paying the price with their lives.

For obvious reasons Naima didn't see many people from those days, but one person she kept in touch with was Truman Crapote. Truman was an eccentric (though thoroughly talentless) teen poet. And, just like Naima during her bleakest moments, he missed his high school life. He never stopped talking about how great life had been when they'd all been in Enkadar! As far as Naima was concerned, this was the very definition of selective memory; Truman had hated his time at high school.

"Do you like my new top hat?"

Truman was also a hopeless fashion victim. He would become dizzy if forced to wear one colour. He had taken to dressing up like an old man from the Victorian era, complete with weird top hat. It looked ridiculous, even for Truman.

"No," Naima said as she savagely pushed the pram forward. "It looks stupid."

He didn't like that comment one bit, but he didn't want to lose the one friend he had from those days, so he remained quiet. Truman had no siblings or family other than his mother. His other friends were chargrilled memories, specters of the bomb; the result of a fantasy gone fatally out of control.

"So," Truman asked carefully, "have you had any strange phone calls recently?"

Naima didn't want to tell Truman that Kai didn't allow

her to use her phone for outbound calls. In fact Kai would probably kill her if he knew she was out with Truman. Kai had a terrible jealous streak. It was irrational, but something to fear. He wouldn't understand that Truman wasn't a threat, he would just see Naima with a man – and then lose control. It wasn't his fault. It was stressful providing for his family.

"My phone hasn't stopped ringing…" Truman continued helpfully.

Naima received a lot of phone calls too, but they were mostly from debt collectors.

Truman stopped Naima and the pram in the middle of the street, a few steps away from the corner shop that wasn't actually on a corner.

"It was her, Naima. It was The Empress!"

The baby started to cry.

***

Naima couldn't sleep if Kai wasn't next to her in bed. It wasn't the most comfy bed (it was a donation from Kai's grandmother and it stank of pee) but that wasn't the reason for Naima's insomnia. The reason she couldn't sleep was because of the memories. They were high-definition memories that morphed into nightmares if she fell asleep – so the best way to avoid the past was for Naima to stay awake. She would pinch her arm and pray that the pain would keep sleep at bay...but it didn't always work.

Kai's reassuring presence kept the past firmly in the past. Kai filled Naima's head and body with distractions. But not even Kai was strong enough to withstand The Empress. The reminders were everywhere regardless of Naima's attempts to distance herself from everything: in the shape of a memorial plaque on the street, on the lips of people pushing trolleys in the supermarket.

And now the local paper was inviting old friends to get back together.

"Whoever put that advert in the local rag is going to get their head kicked in," Naima muttered sluggishly. Kai didn't stir. Naima was allowed to remember the past.

And the past was a tin lunchbox of fire.

***

The day Naima met Truman Crapote – the same day he told her about his strange phone call – became the same night Naima finally fell asleep. Exhausted with trying to keep up with the demands of her newborn baby and run her flat to Kai's approval, Naima's usual coffee-with-two-teaspoons-of-white-gear (it was cheaper than sugar) didn't keep her awake. Sleep was unavoidable.

Naima slept soundly in bed alongside Kai until a fist punched her awake.

"Answer it," Kai said between gritted teeth.

Sluggishly Naima sat up, only to see a mobile telephone

being held under her nose. The screen flashed Unknown Number and the sickly glow from it illuminated Kai's furious brow. He wasn't happy that someone he didn't recognise was trying to reach his girlfriend. Naima shakily took her telephone out of Kai's grip (the first time she'd been allowed to use her phone all day) and answered it.

"Hello?"

Silence and breathing and then a voice:

"Hello, darling!"

Naima jumped out of the bed in shock.

She knew the voice on the other end. It was an impossible voice.

"I'm back," the voice said cheerily.

"Who is it?" Kai snarled sleepily. "Are you cheating on me?"

The voice giggled on the other end.

"He isn't invited to Enkadar. Our world is not for him."

"Who is it?!" Kai was yelling now.

"I'm back," the telephone said. *"The Artist is about to create a new Masterpiece!"*

"You are not back!" Naima shouted hysterically.

"Shhh," said the Endless Empress mockingly. *"You'll wake the baby."*

Naima pinched her arm – but she was wide awake and living in the Real World.

SMACK Y'R ENEMIES WITH CHIPS & CURRY SAUCE

Portia Penelope Pinkerton, now thirteen years old, was trapped in school...but she knew how to escape the daily drudgery. She could *daydream* her way out of prison. It was lunchtime – and though her body was physically in the canteen with everyone else, her mind was wandering deep in the fantasy world of Enkadar.

But she didn't travel alone. She took some friends with her.

***

Portia and her five friends were sitting in the stately palace of Enkadar. The enormous palace windows revealed an endless blue sky. Two enormous dragons circled the palace, smoke billowing from their snorting nostrils, creating swirling patterns in the sky. They were ready for battle. These dragons would kill to defend the people of Enkadar.

The Citizens of Enkadar sat at the large gold desk. Their glorious nation's flag – which displayed a unicorn – was proudly draped across every wall in the golden palace.

The Endless Empress stood and cleared her throat, her eyes darting from person to person. She took in

Commander Carly, Naima Supreme, Captain Quirk, Truman Crapote, and Beehive Betty – and she smiled at each and every one of them.

They waited anxiously to hear what Her Holiness had to say. She was due to make an important announcement. She was planning something spectacular. It was an event that would make Enkadar the hot topic of discussion with everyone.

But Portia didn't get a chance to speak.

Someone launched an unprovoked attack on The Empress.

A missile flew across the room and smacked her on the face; hot and smelly, it dripped off her cheek and plopped onto the floor.

A paper plate of chips and curry sauce!

"We're under attack!" Naima Supreme yelled at the others.

"Commence battle formation!" Commander Carly cried out in a panic.

Everyone knew the drill, and fell to the floor, tipping over their table to create a barricade against the stinky artillery. Portia fell first, crying out in humiliation; the twin dragons outside, defenders of the nation, roared and shimmered away back into a dream. They were powerless against this particular assault.

The royal palace, a shared fantasy, melted away, reverting to the school canteen. It was lunchtime at Castlekrankie High School. Not even the power of teenage imagination could completely overcome bad school lunches.

"Are you okay?" Naima asked, as everyone in the canteen pointed and laughed.

Portia, however, was trembling with anger.

"They won't get away with this!"

"What are you going to do to them?" Commander Carly enquired eagerly.

Portia was about to respond, until a sloppy piece of caramel cake doused in thick custard dropped on her head. She took a deep breath, and burst into tears.

"I have a gun..." she gasped between sobs.

***

MOLLY: Did she have a gun? Or was it just one of her fantasies?
CARLY: No, she had a real gun.
MOLLY: And what did she do with it?
CARLY: She held a classroom hostage.

***

This time Portia had gone too far. This was an entirely different level of lunacy to what everyone at school was used to...because somehow, against all odds, Portia Pinkerton did as she had promised: she somehow managed to get her hands on a gun.

"What *is* she doing?" Carly gasped from the back of the classroom. Beehive Betty, sitting in the row in front of Carly, howled with laughter. Their art teacher, a kindly man named Mr Lake, had left a few minutes beforehand to get some supplies.

But a precious few minutes was all Portia needed in order to ambush the sheep.

She stood before them in full Endless Empress mode, dressed in what could only be described as a military uniform. There was an elaborate purple sash around her shoulders, courtesy of Beehive Betty's creativity with fabric. Black sunglasses obscured Portia's eyes, giving her a detached skull-like expression. Her hair was tied back into a severe but detailed knot. And her polished black boots enabled her to tower over everyone cowering in the classroom.

Portia looked brilliant, absurd, and absolutely terrifying.

"Let's sit back and enjoy the show," Beehive Betty cackled.

But the smirk vanished from Betty's face when The Empress demanded everyone sing the national anthem of Enkadar. This was **not** part of the plan.

***

It didn't appear on any map, and it couldn't be reached by aeroplane or boat or any other conventional means. And yet it was there, this undiscovered country, inside their imaginations. And it *was* real for them. They all believed in it completely: The Empress, Commander Carly, Beehive Betty, Naima Supreme, Captain Quirk and Truman Crapote stood apart from everyone else at school. They didn't belong there with the others, they belonged in Enkadar.

Gaining entry into the glorious paradise of Enkadar was straightforward enough. Escaping it was another thing altogether.

***

MOLLY: Could you clarify something really obvious for me?

CARLY: Of course! What do you want to know?

MOLLY: What *is* Enkadar, exactly?

CARLY: Enkadar is a place of peace. There's no racism, bullies or adults making us feel like crap. It's where The Empress was born.

MOLLY: But?

CARLY: Enkadar isn't real. It only exists inside Portia's imagination.

MOLLY: It used to exist inside *your* imagination too. Didn't it?

CARLY: I'm not like that anymore.

MOLLY: Why would anyone want to live in a pretend country? It makes no sense!

CARLY: We all fell into the fantasy for different reasons.

(Silence)

CARLY: I think she's still there…still lost in the depths of that place.

***

A lone voice of reason squeaked up from the front of the classroom. Both Carly and Betty rolled their eyes at the same time; the voice belonged to Scotty Manduche – a particularly irritating beanpole whose trousers never seemed to fit his spindly legs. And now he was openly contradicting The Empress of Enkadar.

To contradict Her Holiness ranked as a #1 Crime in Enkadar.

"I have top marks in Geography," Scotty said conceitedly. "And I can assure you that no country by the name of Enkadar exists."

The Endless Empress swung around and ferociously cracked Scotty in the face with her pistol. The blow was aggressive enough to send him tottering onto the cold laminate floor. She then aimed the gun at her audience. They were going to sing the national anthem of Enkadar whether they wanted to or not.

The classroom suddenly came together in song. Most

people stumbled over the national anthem – the lyrics of which had been composed over a bowl of Weetabix earlier that morning – but, with Portia's prompting, the sheep eventually united to sing about the awesome glory of Enkadar.

This was a true victory against the oppressive Real World.

"This is the happiest moment of my life," The Empress declared joyfully.

Her happiness was to be short-lived.

***

Mr Lake returned with some canvases tucked underarm to discover his pupils singing a song to a fictional country and Portia holding a toy gun.

"Is that gun a fake?" he said in disbelief.

"YES!" Beehive Betty called out from the far end of the room.

The singing abruptly stopped.

And the riot started.

HOW TO BE A KICKASS JOURNALIST IN CASTLEKRANKIE
The Hunt for the Endless Empress

Molly considered herself a skillful journalist, and though she was currently unemployed, she kept herself motivated with the knowledge that **one big story could change everything**. This story was THE ONE. It would pay her rent forever. Molly shuddered at the thought of working in a factory or supermarket. She considered herself too talented. It would be degrading!

Besides, Molly thought slyly, *I have a calling and a mission. This isn't just a story for a newspaper; it's a means to an end.*

Carly, without prompting, suddenly displayed a frightening flash of insight. Molly realised that this was to become a common occurrence for the strange girl.

"Which paper did you say you worked for again?"

"*The Castlekrankie Chronicle*," Molly replied slickly.

"No," Carly corrected her, "you don't."

Molly reached across the table to switch off her Dictaphone. The battery was precious and she didn't want to waste it on debates about her employment history.

"Proper journalists use notepads, not tape recorders," Carly added, whilst studying a fascinating stain on the shredded tablecloth.

"Excuse me?" Molly said, insulted. This wasn't the first time her professional standards had been called into question. It certainly wouldn't be the last.

"I said proper journalists use notepads, not tape recorders. You have a note pad. You scribble on it. You should use shorthand like a real investigative journalist."

One of the waitresses across the far side of the café (the peroxide grouch) found the exchange very amusing. She covered her face with her white hair to hide her glee. Molly shot her a vicious glance, before turning her ire against the interviewee. The urge to slap Carly across the face overwhelmed Molly for a second, but she had to humour the mad girl in order to get a scoop.

It was apparent Molly wasn't the only one at the table to have done her research.

I've underestimated her, Molly realised.

Molly decided on a unique new interview approach:

She decided to be honest.

"I'm currently looking for work and I'm hoping your story will get me some attention. I previously worked for *The Castlekrankie Chronicle*. But the recent cutbacks resulted in my redundancy. I'm now freelance. I don't use shorthand because I don't think it's a reliable way of conducting an interview. Is that okay?"

Carly nodded appreciatively at being treated with some respect.

"You'll be the most famous journalist in the world after your write this story."

Molly felt her breath catch deep in her chest. The idea of having editors begging her to work at their publications was startlingly seductive.

Carly turned and politely asked the waitress for another pot of tea. The waitress rolled her eyes but did her job, despite clearly hating every second of it.

A reenergised Molly decided to press on with her interview.

"I'm going to read you a list of names from your days at school. I'd like you to provide some sound bites about them."

"Which names?"

"Former Citizens of Enkadar…are you ready to hear their names?" Molly asked.

Carly twice nodded her agreement. YES. YES.

Molly started:

"Richard Crampshee."

"Captain Quirk. He's dead."

"Truman Stanza."

"Truman Crapote! Avoid his poetry recitals at all costs."

"Naima Calmar."

"Naima Supreme. She completely lost it at the trial. I haven't seen her in years. I don't think she coped well in the aftermath of…well, the funerals."

Molly scribbled all of this down – long-hand – onto her pad.

"Elizabeth McNab."

"That's Beehive Betty, The Hairspray Queen. She had

bright ginger hair which she hated, so she wore a big black beehive wig. She sprayed it into shape every day."

A breath, a heartbeat, a thought, a middle eight:

"I didn't attend Betty's funeral. The police wouldn't provide protection against the crowds. Besides, I would have been a hypocrite going to her funeral."

Carly stopped speaking again and closed her eyes, momentarily rocked by a rush of feelings and thoughts only she could interpret. Then she came back to life with a sad little smile on her face. Molly could see that Carly didn't smile very often.

"They were my friends," Carly started up.

Now we're getting to the good stuff, Molly thought hungrily.

Secretly, surreptitiously, she reached over and pressed RECORD.

***

MOLLY: You joined Portia's cult. Tell me about it.
CARLY: We were the Citizens of Enkadar. We used to make believe we were rock stars, princesses, famous celebrities. We dressed up!
MOLLY: Fancy dress?
CARLY: Yeah! Portia once told me she would rather people looked at her in shock than pity. You won't understand that until I tell you the rest of our story.

MOLLY: When did your little gang decide to murder everyone at school?

***

The blonde waitress slammed a teapot down onto the table with enough force to shake it. The Dictaphone trembled, and not for the first time did Molly wish Carly had chosen somewhere else for their interview. Everything about the café was utterly nauseating; from the food to the décor...but the worst thing was the insolent staff. Molly turned towards the café owner. She wanted to complain about his waitress, but stopped when she witnessed something utterly sickening:

The man behind the counter was in the midst of picking his nose.

Molly McCrumb, journalist extraordinaire, recoiled in disgust. She decided to concentrate on her mission; anything to take her mind off of her surroundings. She couldn't understand why Carly had brought her to this hellish place for an interview!

"I have one last name to give you," Molly said indistinctly.

"Wonderful!" Carly cried out. She was transfixed by the digital Dictaphone.

"Portia Penelope Pinkerton."

"Ah," Carly exclaimed, "Her Holiness the Endless Empress of Enkadar!"

Molly already knew that, of course.

"You do realize that the others won't talk," Carly said as she lifted the pot of tea.

"I can be very determined when I want something," Molly replied calmly. "Did you see that strange notice in the newspaper? It advertised a reunion for your old gang."

Carly ignored the question. She preferred discussing Portia.

Molly didn't know what else to do, and so she added to her notes as Carly spoke.

"Portia's parents died this year. They were very religious. And they gave Portia a peculiar single-mindedness, which is a fine quality for an uncompromising extremist."

"How did Portia's parents die?"

"I think they died of broken hearts. Or embarrassment?" Carly replied oddly.

Carly was full of these peculiar and cryptic statements, in fact entire conversations would start and end with some impenetrable comment. Carly's oddest remark, however, was to be delivered in her usual fractured manner:

"You do realise that The Empress is planning another Masterpiece."

Carly reached over to the sugar jar and deliberately tipped it over.

***

CARLY: I'm so clumsy! I've spilled this sugar all over the table! How dumb of me!

MOLLY: If you know something and you don't tell me – it will make you an accessory to a crime. Do you really want that to happen to you again?

(Carly laughs)

MOLLY: What is The Empress planning?

***

"What is The Empress planning?" Molly asked again with determination.

Carly didn't reply except to point down at the table. Molly looked down at the mess caused by the tipped out sugar jar. The Dictaphone couldn't record it, but Carly had used a finger to etch one word into the sodden sugary white mess:

CARLY COSTELLO'S HOSPITAL HOLIDAY

Carly Costello was engaged in a battle of wits with her Conscience. Every single day, at various times, she would get letters from her Conscience. They weren't postmarked, which meant her Conscience lived locally. But it was extremely frustrating, because Carly didn't want to read what her Conscience had to say.

Whenever Carly threatened to move on with her life, whenever she got close to finding a job, her Conscience would send her new workmates poison pen letters. These letters, always in green envelopes, would tell Carly's workmates about the 'mass murderer' lurking in the office.

Carly didn't keep jobs for long.

No matter where Carly moved, her Conscience would find her and write more letters. They were always full of venom and rage and grief.

It wasn't The Empress. That she knew for a fact. But who was it?

Carly decided she needed a good old-fashioned holiday: somewhere classy and remote, somewhere with fine dining and attentive staff who would attend her every need.

So Carly decided to book herself into the local hospital for a few weeks.

It was okay – she'd been there many times in the past.

"I am not ready to leave yet," Carly whispered from her hospital bed. She was too scared to face the public and her home wasn't safe from the outside world. From the safety of her hospital bed, she plotted revenge against The Endless Empress. Yes, the nurses knew all about Enkadar and all of that stuff – everyone did thanks to the newspapers constantly running stories about the massacre. But the hospital staff weren't allowed to say anything about it. Hospital was a horrible place full of spluttering pensioners, but they were too ill to bother about Carly's past affiliations. Carly shrank into her bed as dark thoughts assailed her. She looked around with a methodical eye. The place was absolutely filthy with grime! It soon became obvious that she would be lucky to escape the ward uncontaminated.

Perhaps that was Portia's plan all along? Massacre innocent people, disappear, and then ensure her former friends took nervous breakdowns so they ended up in hospital. An infection from a dirty ward might succeed where stress had not.

Carly hadn't eaten solid food for weeks. It was high school all over again. She had come out of that nightmare feeling strong and in control of her own destiny, until someone put that stupid advert in the local newspaper. *The Masterpiece was nearly four years ago*, Carly thought bitterly. *Why won't people leave me alone?*

It took a few days of bed-ridden contemplation but it happened in due course. A plan came together, and suddenly everything didn't seem so bleak. Purpose took hold of Carly. It was powerful enough to replace her sense of despair.

But first she needed to escape her hospital holiday and all the germs in the ward.

***

It was a few weeks into her hospital holiday when The Conscience found Carly again. She was lying content in bed, watching a quiz show on the old TV, when the postman arrived with the morning mail. Miserable and grouchy (because his wages were being slashed), he threw a familiar green envelope down at Portia.

Predictably, there was a letter bearing the name CARLY COSTELLO on it.

She ripped it open with trembling fingers and read the words of a crazy pen.

***

DEAR CARLY,

When are you going to do the right thing and kill The Endless Empress?

KILLERS KILL KILLERS KILL KILLERS KILL KILLERS KILL

The agony I feel is Endless just like your mad Empress. I cry every day because of you and your friends. Do the patients know there's a killer here with them?

KILLER HERE! KILLer HERe! KILL HER!

Pleasepleasepleasepleasepleasekillher. Kill The Empress! Do it for me.

PS When you've killed The Empress, please kill yourself too.

I'M WATCHING YOU KILLER.

YOURS SINCERELY,

Someone with a CONSCIENCE

***

The day after the letter started with an innocent question:

"Why are you so damn lazy?"

It was an innocent query but one Carly needed answered.

The Nurse feigned disbelief at her patient's impertinence.

"You are not allowed to speak to me with that tone of voice!"

The Nurse always entered the ward flanked by her domestic staff. Every day she would let the domestic staff do all the hard work. The hard work at the hospital, it seemed, did not include cleaning the ward appropriately.

"You should set an example to your staff, and be a supportive superior," Carly lectured in her most pompous tone. She was trying to do an impression – for that was how The Endless Empress came across during a good rant.

The domestics laid out plates for all patients excluding those with beds marked Nil by Mouth. Not all of the patients were happy to be fed hospital food. One of them, an old lady two beds down from Carly, shouted:

"I don't want your damn carrots!"

The Nurse scooped up the old lady's carrots onto her hand and swallowed them voraciously.

"Carrots are lovely with butter on them."

Carly was furious at what she'd just witnessed.

"Shouldn't you encourage your patients to *eat* all of their food instead of grubbing on it yourself?" Carly asked curtly.

The Nurse was first startled by the criticism, and then alarmed by it because she knew Carly was absolutely right. She had no idea she was being so closely observed. The Nurse ate quite a lot of food from the plates of her patients.

"Well," the Nurse replied snippily, "you could try eating your own food!"

Carly gasped. It was a low blow.

***

Why did she do it? The Empress didn't one day decide to blow up a school because she thought it would be fun. No. The Citizens did bad things until the idea of doing the bad things seemed like a *good* thing. The Masterpiece ruined lives and scarred an entire generation. But its effect on the survivors was just as catastrophic. Carly felt the pressure more than most because of her childhood friendship with The Empress. She couldn't leave her house because she was too scared to walk out in public. She hated life. She hated herself. And she hated food. Her Conscience would call her names like FAT COW and UGLY TROLL and OBESE BEAST. Sometimes Carly read the letters and imagined her mother saying the words, because it all sounded like stuff her mother said to her every day. Her mother, skinny and proud, would mark everything in the fridge with eyeliner, just so she could check how much Carly ate at night.

And yet Carly became a new person when she stopped eating. She became thinner, and she suddenly felt a sense of power previously absent from her chaotic life.

When Carly eventually caught a nasty bout of the flu, she thought nothing of it and coughed and coughed...until her pelvis broke down the middle. That's when she first heard the word 'bulimia' used to describe her condition. She had enjoyed many hospital holidays since her initial diagnosis.

The hospital was the only solution to her problem.

That – and plotting revenge – helped Carly survive the wreckage of her life.

***

With a plan fully formed inside her head, Carly decided to write some notes in order to pass the time. Carly liked lists. A list made sense of the muddle. Carly sat on her bed drafting a few ideas and ticking off uncertainties. In a matter of days she put her missing weight back on and food was no longer a minor inconvenience.

Carly finally read over her completed list.

The list detailed her lost friends. Some were still alive. Some were not.

CARLY'S LIST

1   *Carly Costello AKA Commander Carly. Status: bored.*
2   *Richard Crampshee AKA Captain Quirk. Status:* **dead.**
3   *Truman Stanza AKA Truman Crapote. Status: alive.*
4   *Elizabeth McNab AKA Beehive Betty, the Hairspray Queen. Status:* **dead.**
5   *Naima Calmar AKA Naima Supreme. Status: alive.*

Carly wrote down the final and most important name on the list.

6   *Portia Penelope Pinkerton AKA the Endless Empress AKA the Artist AKA Pinko AKA the Butcher of Castlekrankie High School AKA Revolution Girl AKA Her Holiness, the Endless Empress of Enkadar. Status: Alive!*

Then, as an afterthought, Carly altered the last bit of the list:

Status: DEAD WHEN I FIND HER!

***

Molly peered over the list and felt herself blaze red with excitement.

"Yes," Carly said with a mischievous glint in her black eyes, "I mean it."

A VISION OF TRUE BEAUTY
IN FIFTH PERIOD

Captain Quirk was a lively creative youth who fell in with Portia's gang because he didn't fit in anywhere else. He didn't even feel at home in his actual home. A science fiction aficionado who could speak fluent geek, Quirk knew nothing of actual people, and so he became a Citizen of Enkadar almost by default.

This is the story of how Captain Quirk fell under the power of the Endless Empress.

***

Quirk's problems started with his name. It was the worst name in the world! Richard Crampshee just wasn't a sexy name. 'Richard Crampshee' announced nothing other than HEY I'M A GEEK AND I JUST CAN'T WAIT TO BE BULLIED. And the school bullies responded to the challenge with eagerness; they wasted no time in calling Richard the pocket-sized version of his forename:

And what name is short for Richard? Dick. Yes. Dick. Dick Crampshee.

Quirk's surname was just as bad as his forename. Crampshee! Richard actually hated his second name more than his first name. Captain Quirk knew that 'Cramp' was something a woman suffered from during her "time of the month", thus his name was linked to women's problems. Crampshee also has the word 'she' in it.

Quirk hated his name nearly as much as he hated himself.

His main problem, however, was that he actually wanted to be called Jackie.

***

In a bid to toughen up his wimpy son, Mr Crampshee decided to train him in the art of boxing. Quirk dreaded his mother leaving for one of her jobs, because as soon as the door closed behind her…Mr Crampshee pulled out the boxing gloves. He led his son into the basement and trained him vigorously. This training consisted of Mr Crampshee beating his son up, until he fell into a heap on the floor.

The broken nose was an accident. Mr Crampshee didn't mean to snap it.

One day, their sparring went even further than just a broken nose.

Captain Quirk, sick and tired of being battered, threw a lucky punch and hit his father on the face. It was one time only. But Mr Crampshee punched back…and he didn't stop until his son was out cold. There was only one problem:

Captain Quirk wasn't breathing.

Terrified that his wife would find out about their sessions in the basement, Mrs Crampshee took his son to hospital. It was there he begged him not to say anything.

Father and son hugged, reaching a true understanding.

Nothing was ever said to Mr Crampshee.

Quirk left hospital and training resumed two days later.

***

Captain Quirk was plain old Richard Crampshee until he met Portia Penelope Pinkerton. But Quirk knew there was something special about the girl as soon as he looked at her. Portia carried herself in a way that suggested superiority; she knew she was greater than all the mundane people of the world. He'd heard rumours about her too; that she liked to torture animals, that she enjoyed cutting herself.

That she was absolutely crazy.

***

Captain Quirk met Portia in Art, fifth period, Thursday.

They were painting, of course.

"You look like Jesus," Portia said crisply. Captain Quirk thought about his appearance, and realised that maybe Portia wasn't far wrong. He had long hair, thick and brown, dangling almost down to his shoulders. He wore beads, just like a hippy – and these things clearly translated to a Jesus lookalike in Portia's reckoning.

"You're new here, aren't you?" Quirk asked.

"No," Portia said with a look of dissatisfaction. "I've been here as long as you."

Captain Quirk didn't answer, because he had suddenly noticed something on Portia's arms: large, painful burn marks. Her snagged sleeve betrayed something personal, something she had tried to hide for years.

"What happed to your arm?" Quirk asked nosily.

"What happened to your nose?" Portia retorted.

Captain Quirk suddenly felt the old ache, but he said nothing.

An awkward silence filled the air between the two teenagers.

Then, without any announcement, Portia flicked red paint at Quirk's canvas. He tried to laugh, to show her he had a sense of humour. But he was annoyed and couldn't hide it.

"Why did you do that?" Quirk snapped irritably.

"Because I'm crazy," she laughed.

Quirk decided to teach the girl a lesson by wrecking her painting. He dipped his brush into a tub of yellow, and then prepared to launch it at the portrait. But when Quirk looked over at Portia's painting, he nearly fell to his knees in awe:

It was the most beautiful thing Quirk had ever seen in his life.

"What is it?" he gasped, dropping the yellow stained brush.

"It's a place inside my head," Portia told him with pride. "I call it Enkadar."

And that's how they became friends.

***

It was a rare day of sunshine in Castlekrankie, so Portia and Quirk took time out to lie on the grassy knoll, near the snake bridge that separated school from the housing district. (The snake bridge was yet another quirky piece of architecture found in Castlekrankie). It twisted into a wobbly shape – thus the 'snake' nickname. They looked down on everyone, pupils at school weaving around like little microbes under a bright spotlight. Some adults passed by, but they didn't say anything. A postman did, however, give Quirk the thumbs up.

He clearly thought the two teens were out on a date, but Portia wasn't Quirk's type.

"I see things, you know," Portia told The Captain.

She wore her school uniform, but the logo embroidered on her chest had been vandalised to read Enkadar High School. Quirk thought that was a brilliant move.

Portia was relieved to see her new friend smile with understanding.

"I like to pretend I'm adopted," Quirk explained. "My real dad is a starship captain."

He closed his eyes, felt the heat, and waited for Portia's response:

"What's wrong with your Real World mum and dad?"

"There's nothing wrong with mum, except she can't see what's happening right under her nose." Captain Quirk brushed his fingers across his own nose. He was admitting to someone – for the first time – the darkness in his life. "My dad beats me. He's violent. And he wastes his life in the pub. Do you know what I mean?"

Portia knew exactly what Captain Quirk meant.

And she vowed to do something about it.

***

Mr Crampshee died in a bizarre accident two weeks later. He was leaving the pub, drunk and rowdy, when he fell down a steep flight of stone stairs. There had been a warning sign up, but for some reason it wasn't there when Quirk's dad staggered by.

And though the CCTV footage was inconclusive...

It looked as if someone had skipped past Mr Crampshee just before he had fallen to his death.

***

"Imagination is the ultimate weapon," Portia explained. "Come and live in Enkadar!"

Quirk was speechless. He didn't say anything about his

dad's death. He didn't want to admit his suspicions. But Portia's words captured him body and soul, providing him with something he lacked…a sense of purpose…a *need* of some sort. Quirk knew above all things that he would do anything to live in the world of Enkadar, because Quirk wanted to be part of something exciting. He didn't want to be a member of the herd anymore. Quirk wanted to see the great nation of Enkadar.

He wanted to visit the halcyon corridors of Portia's imagination.

He wanted to lock himself into something glorious.

***

Richard Crampshee's need to belong would ultimately lead to his death.

But you know that already, don't you?

SHOPPING BAGS OF DOOM
The Hunt for the Endless Empress

Molly didn't smoke, but she *had* to get out of the café. She needed to escape the madness of the interview, so she told Carly that a cigarette break was necessary. After enduring a lecture on the dangers of nicotine (from a suspected bomber!), Molly was finally allowed to leave. Once outside, Molly stood in the peace, sucking in some cool air. She closed her eyes and absorbed the serenity. Her head swirled and her handbag – which she refused to leave – felt heavy on her shoulder.

It'll all be worth it in the end, Molly told herself with tightly shut eyes.

The café was full of customers. Why anyone would choose to spend their free time in Go Joe's was a mystery not even Molly could solve. It was mostly men too. That was a strange observation, but Carly seemed to enjoy being the only girl in the café alongside Molly and the snarky waitress. Oh yes, The Worst Waitress in the World was still there, dropping hints for them to leave – as well as dropping plates and cups.

When Molly finally opened her sore eyes, she did so to a truly bizarre sight:

He stood across the street, watching her intently, a quizzical expression on his face. He was a teenager, possibly seventeen or eighteen years old. His outline blotted out the drab garage doors behind him; he wore an enormous black top hat and tail coat.

His hands held several blue bags, bulging with parcels and groceries.

Molly recognised this strange figure at once. He was a former Citizen of Enkadar.

"Truman Crapote," she said quietly. "I didn't expect to see you here."

"I'm shopping," he replied, his voice a high whistle.

Molly, a journalist used to asking questions, suddenly didn't have any questions to ask. That sort of thing happened every now and again. Truman didn't seem to mind. He was content to wait for Molly to question him. Molly had emailed Truman many times during late nights and early mornings...only to discover he hadn't bothered replying to her. She sometimes screamed with frustration at his discourtesy. She even questioned whether or not she had the correct email address.

Ping! Molly suddenly had her first question:

"Did you get my messages?"

He nodded enthusiastically. Indeed he *had* received her emails. His enormous top hat moved in flawless motion with his head. Molly was slightly resentful – she couldn't wear a hat without it flying off her head at the slightest gust of wind. How did Truman keep his hat secured so snugly?

"I always dress to impress!" he said in rhyme. "Top hat and tails never fail."

***

Molly had read all about Truman's curious condition in the police reports. At the time of the bombing, he had been rounded up with the other living Citizens of Enkadar and questioned under anti-terrorism laws. He was kept in a cell for three days before being freed. One source told Molly that Truman had cried like a baby every single night. Another source said he seemed eerily calm throughout his ordeal. Leaked police reports also mentioned a peculiarity in Truman, a condition known by specialists as **Obsessive Compulsive Rhyming Disorder**:

Truman literally couldn't stop rhyming – and there was no cure for it.

***

"Why are you really here?" Molly asked Truman.

"You won't know what I mean, but the girl in the café isn't what she seems."

Molly looked through the grimy glass café window. Carly was playing with two items of her cutlery, pretending they were a married couple in a fight. Molly already knew that Carly was a formidable foe – she didn't need Truman warning her to be vigilant.

But now he was here, it was the perfect time to get his side of the story.

More details could only help Molly find The Endless Empress.

"Why did you ignore my emails? You can help me write the truth about the bombing, and tell the truth about the Empire of Enkadar. You can't hide forever."

"Forever? Never!" Truman snapped, and then he lowered his voice. He obviously didn't want Carly to know he was outside the café. He placed his hand on Molly's shoulder, and then he gently pulled her away from the grimy surroundings.

"Where are you taking me?" Molly demanded.

"Be as meek as a mouse," Truman replied, "and we'll go to *her* house."

***

We didn't travel far. I recognised many of the places we passed on the way to Portia's childhood home. I was raised in this area but left it a few years ago. I only returned to Castlekrankie to pursue this story. It was unsettling, because everything brought back memories of my family. I had to remind myself that this wasn't about me, I wasn't writing my memoirs. But I would be lying if I didn't admit to having reservations.

It's a strange thing to walk down a street with a suspected murderer. Despite being absurdity in motion, Truman had allegedly taken part in a killing spree that ended the lives of over one thousand teenagers and a scattering of adults.

I wasn't completely comfortable around Truman.

But I was in that cafe to find the facts...no matter where it took me.

And it took me somewhere unexpected.

***

They were loitering outside a wrecked house.

"This is where The Endless Empress grew up," Truman said calmly.

(It was only later that Molly realised he hadn't rhymed that comment.)

The house was pure Castlekrankie, in that it looked like something out of Transylvania, complete with turrets and narrow windows. It was all sharp edges and strange angles. It also looked like someone had set off a bomb inside it – and from what Molly knew of Portia's modus operandi, that was a possibility.

"What happened to this place?" Molly asked gently.

"She departed in a puff of smoke. Destroying the evidence was a masterstroke."

The house was still standing, but only barely. One wall, the facing wall, had a message sprayed onto it that neatly summed up everything the people of Castlekrankie wanted to say about The Endless Empress:

BURN IN HELL PORTIA PINKERTON!

Molly asked the final question:

"Were you involved in The Masterpiece?"

But Truman was gone. He had managed to slip away without Molly noticing. She stood there for a few seconds, stupefied into silence, before remembering that Carly was still waiting for her back at the café, probably still in her little reverie.

Molly walked away from the ruined house towards Go Joe's café.

She walked and walked, uninterrupted in thought, until a bus passed by. It was the X39. There was nothing unusual in a bus driving down a road. After all, Castlekrankie had a good transit system. The driver behind the wheel slowed the bus, albeit temporarily. She waved at Molly from inside the empty bus.

Molly idly waved back. She didn't recognise the driver – a middle-aged woman with fiery auburn hair – but it was always polite to be polite.

***

Carly looked upset when Molly returned to her seat in Go Joe's Café.

She held an envelope in her hands. The envelope was the same colour as Carly's face, a sort of sickly green hue. Molly also observed two things: Carly's makeup was smudged across her cheeks: a sure sign that Carly had recently shed a few tears. Something in the letter had obviously upset her and – not for the first time – Carly looked frightened. Molly also noticed that the envelope wasn't postmarked, which meant it had been hand-delivered while Molly was out with Truman.

"The postman stopped by while you were away," Carly sniffed.

Molly motioned with a nod to the green envelope.

"I assume he delivered your mail?"

"Yes."

"Do you mind if I read your letter?

Carly smiled weakly, but didn't say no.

Molly read over the words on the letter:

***

DEAR CARLY,

I know you still haven't killed The Endless Empress and now I'm getting really angry with you. DO YOU THINK I CAN WAIT FOREVER? I am not endless and I am not forever. I am a normal person with a life. HURRY UP!

DIE! DIE! DIE! DIEt! DIET! DIE!

Stop sitting in that café, Lazybones, and GET OUT and find The Endless Empress.

PS When you've killed The Empress,

please kill yourself too.

I'M WATCHING YOU KILLER.
YOURS SINCERELY,

Someone with a CONSCIENCE

***

"My Conscience is becoming very impatient with me."

Then Carly's mood whiplashed from utter despair to chirpy glee in an instant:

"But at least I didn't eat any sandwiches!"

Molly McCrumb, kickass journalist, took a seat and rejoined the circus.

A LITTLE MORE CONVERSATION, A LITTLE LESS ACTION

Slag. Tramp. Slut. Tart. Naima first heard these words used as an insult at high school. Naima had no idea what she'd done to deserve her reputation, because she hadn't ever been out on a date. The rumours just started, and once a rumour starts... stopping it is nearly impossible. Naima was just a normal teenager with a big imagination – and a bit more pocket money than most people her own age. Her parents had a string of businesses: portable spray tan salons, actually. They worked at the expense of their marriage. Naima's father spent a little bit too long in the office with that lovely new secretary, the one with the blonde hair and tight sweater. And her mother wasn't even her real mother. Naima's stepmother ignored her, preferring instead the company of the gardener. She spent all day and night with him.

His name was Tom and he loved working in Mrs Calmar's garden.

There was only one problem with Naima's mother having a full time gardener:

The Calmar family didn't have a garden.

They lived in a posh flat.

After The Masterpiece, Naima found herself

living a different life in a different flat.

***

Naima had found a useful way of keeping the baby quiet during the day. It was her secret and not even Kai knew anything about it. She simply dosed her baby with a spoonful of SleepEazy in the morning. Drowsiness preceded a deep 'natural' sleep.

Peace, at last, Naima thought in relief. She used her time wisely and set about tracking down The Endless Empress. The phone calls were becoming more and more vicious. Portia often sounded close to the edge of mental disintegration. There was a time when The Empress gave Naima confidence to stand up to bullies, but Portia had become the ultimate bully – and she had to be stopped.

Naima felt some of her old fire returning; and yet she still yelped in fright every time the phone rang in the background. One exceptional phone call nearly went ignored, but Naima eventually summoned the courage to answer it.

It wasn't The Endless Empress.

It was a journalist.

***

"I've been looking for you," the journalist had said pleasantly. "I'm hoping to do a story on the Castlekrankie

High School massacre. It's the three-year anniversary soon and I thought it would be good for you to give your account. The bombing of a school during an award ceremony is a powerful human interest story..."

***

Naima had been warned about this nosy pest. Truman had told Naima about the journalist during one of his sneak visits. Molly McCrumb was, he claimed, a persistent menace. She had spammed his email account for a month. Why were people so obsessed with the past? Naima had to live in the present, and presently...she had no money.

The wallpaper was hanging off, the television still had a crack in it, and the damp on the windows flaked at the slightest disturbance.

The house was a damn mess.

Naima made her mind up. She didn't care anymore. She needed money!

***

"Will I get paid for my interview?" Naima asked the journalist.

There was a lengthy silence from the other end of the line.

Finally, at last, the journalist agreed to pay her for the story of a lifetime.

"I'll meet you tomorrow at The Wishing Well inside the shopping mall," Naima added, suddenly embarrassed at her desperation. "I'll bring Princess with me, but don't worry about any noise. I have a feeling she'll be in a deep natural sleep."

Naima looked over at the bottle of SleepEazy on the table; the story she had to tell the journalist was so lengthy that Princess would probably require a few extra doses.

**

The next day was fraught with all sorts of hidden horrors. Kai nearly took the day off from his new job at Planet Pound to spend it with Naima. He had been assigned to the discount store after being threatened with a cut in his dole money. But the hours were bizarre! Sometimes he would work late at night – even when Planet Pound was closed. He explained that the warehouse was still open and that he was doing everything for Naima.

"You're an ungrateful little slag," Kai snarled as he walked out the door.

A moist mouldy mist fluttered past Naima's face and suddenly, both sickened and empowered, she packed the pram with the essentials for taking a baby out: nappies, cream, bottles of milk and most importantly...a bottle of SleepEazy.

***

The Wishing Well had been funded by the local council association. They had used money left over from the closure of libraries. It was a piece of modern art for a town without any imagination. Some people wanted horse heads, others wanted water maidens, but they could only afford a wishing well. People threw only copper coins into the well because pound coins vanished into the pockets of drifting drug addicts. The well was situated inside the shopping mall and was almost completely dry, mostly thanks to a problem with the pipes – they were blocked with used syringes.

Naima waited patiently, rocking the pram back and forth in a bid to look natural, although her baby was so deeply asleep that it was a futile gesture.

The mall was heaving with shoppers and Naima didn't want to be recognised. But the shoppers seemed more concerned about the *BIG SALE* than Naima. There was also a talented mime artist doing a moonwalk in front of the bemused public; he was dressed in an elaborate Elvis jumpsuit, complete with big sunglasses and huge sideburns. Naima felt sick with fear at the idea of being discovered in public. She would be lynched due to her association with The Endless Empress.

Elvis was proving to be a useful distraction.

"Where is that damn journalist?" Naima muttered fiercely.

She waited and waited until suddenly...at long last someone walked out of the crowd towards her! Naima felt relief as she took in the approaching person's huge grin.

But it wasn't a journalist moving in her direction.

It was Elvis. He was dancing a classic Elvis dance, and the shoppers were beguiled. They cheered him on, encouraging him to pull ever more ridiculous dance moves. But if the mime artist wanted money for his hard work, he'd have to look elsewhere. Naima was only meeting up with the journalist so she could buy new wallpaper. She had no money in her purse or her bank account. Kai took all the money for his own account. As the man of the house, it was his responsibility to protect Naima's finances.

Elvis removed his sunglasses and clear blue eyes flashed triumphantly.

"Are you on gear or something?" Elvis snickered.

Naima's red-rimmed eyes nearly popped out of her skull.

"Do I know you?" she snapped.

"No," Elvis replied, "but we have a mutual friend."

Naima's throat dried up, because she knew what was coming next.

"Her Holiness has ordered me to keep an eye on you," Elvis said, whilst in a pose.

"Tell The Empress to go and drown herself in the wishing well behind me!"

Naima's open defiance of The Empress shook Elvis up, and he put his hands on his hips. Naima couldn't really see his face, because of the enormous sunglasses perched on his nose. But he was definitely Portia's spokesman. Her voice was his voice.

"We're fighting an evil force. Enkadar is still at war with Milordahl."

Naima had heard the fanatical rhetoric many times in the past.

Indeed she used to speak just like the Elvis impersonator.

"And how is the war effort going?"

Elvis smiled.

"We're going to bomb this world into a bloody mess."

**

Milordahl! Naima hadn't heard that word used since high school. Milordahl is Portia's imaginary name for the Real World. For normal people, it's Planet Earth or The World. But to Portia and the Citizens of Enkadar, the Real World will always be known as Milordahl.

The Real World is incompatible with Portia's fantasy world – so one of them has to go. And for that reason, the cold war between Enkadar and Milordahl will never end. The war, just like everything else about Enkadar, is a product of Portia's warped imagination.

But chillingly...Portia believes in it completely.

And Naima, for her shame, once believed in it too.

***

Naima suddenly understood that there was no journalist coming to meet her.

She was caught in a trap set by Portia.

"You lured me here," Naima said numbly, and not just because the gear had kicked in. Then another black thought came out of obscurity, to the fore:

What if Kai discovered she had gone out without his permission?

"There *is* a journalist," Elvis told her. "Her name is Molly McCrumb. Her Holiness wants you to stay away from her. The journalist is not to be trusted."

"What's Portia's problem with her?" Naima was scared for the poor journalist.

"Miss Molly is hunting for my employer. As if you can track down a God!"

Fear of Kai evaporated temporarily to be replaced by indignation.

Then, as an aside, Naima uttered a bold lie:

"I'm not afraid of The Empress anymore."

Elvis shrugged, and then tilted his head in the direction behind Naima.

What is he trying to show me?

A familiar figure – one she knew intimately – stood at the other end of the mall.

But what was he doing here when he was meant to be at work?

"Kai!" Naima called out to her boyfriend. "Kai!"

He didn't hear her.

He was too busy kissing another girl.

"Her Holiness decided it was best for you to know what he's doing to you."

"Why?"

But Naima already knew what Elvis was going to say before he opened his mouth:

"Her Holiness wants you to return to Enkadar. It's where you belong."

Naima turned away from the painful sight of her boyfriend's public infidelity. Her fury was now directed at the man in fancy dress. She wanted to kill him.

But it was too late:

Elvis had already left the building.

TEEN GANGS MUST RRRRULE!

Before they made a bomb, they made a pact.

***

The brick wall was a rogue's gallery of school bullies. Each face in each portrait seemed menacing. Some were girls, but most were boys. They all had one thing in common: at some point during their high school lives, each had somehow tormented or bullied a Citizen of Enkadar.

And if the faces on the wall could have seen with real eyes, they would have been able to watch Captain Quirk swearing his sacred oath to the gang of Enkadar. He stood in the centre of The Embassy, his right hand raised high, nearly as high as his head. The others stood around him: The Endless Empress, The Hairspray Queen, Commander Carly, Naima Supreme and Truman Crapote. Their backs were turned to the wall.

Everyone else had sworn the sacred oath, and now it was Captain Quirk's turn.

"And I swear that I will uphold the fantasy of Enkadar even when I am told it is not real. I swear to stay here forever and ever and ever. I will protect it against those who wish to violate the sanctity of the construct..."

Quirk, the newest member of the group, tried his best –

but he stumbled on the sacred oath. This was unfortunate, because the writer of the oath happened to be standing behind him. Truman could only watch with horror as Quirk bungled the ceremonial vow. The fun they were having would have to come to an abrupt end, because he wasn't doing it the right way: or rather, he wasn't doing it *Portia's* way.

"And I swear that I will uphold...erm...Enkadar even when I am told it isn't real. I swear to stay here. I will protect it against those...erm...violate the construct..."

"NO!" Portia Penelope Pinkerton stamped her feet. "You're doing it all wrong!"

Truman glared ominously at Portia, because she had just robbed him of his moment. It was *his* speech. He'd written it just for *this* moment, so *he* should have been the one to correct the newest citizen to Enkadar. Besides, this was *his* Embassy.

"Could we hurry this up?" Beehive Betty, the Hairspray Queen, said in the background. "I'm going out with my sister tonight, and she doesn't 'get' the whole Enkadar thing."

***

MOLLY: Where was The Enkadarian Embassy anyway?
CARLY: In Enkadar, obviously.
MOLLY: Yes, I get that...but where was it really?
CARLY: Oh! How silly of me. It was the attic at the top

of Truman's house.

***

"My demonstration with the fake gun didn't work. We are still being bullied. And now the teachers are persecuting us too. No-one takes us seriously!"

Beehive Betty, busy spraying her wig into shape, spoke up:

"The teachers are all sexist, horrible jerks. We should have photographs of them up on the bully wall! Do you notice how they ask girls questions about *Pride and Prejudice* but ask the boys questions about *1984*. Sexism is illegal in Enkadar!"

Everyone coughed in harmony, while being smothered with hairspray fumes.

***

The Citizens had drafted up a Bill of Rights a few months before Captain Quirk had joined their gang. And one of their laws did indeed state: *We Shall Not Be Sexist Pigs like the Teachers at Castlekrankie High School.* I should know. I've read them. Forty pages of the most random laws any country – real or unreal – could create.

Did you know that it's illegal to wear polyester in Enkadar? And that all Citizens must wear the colour purple during the month of Vandoreen. And if you should be caught reading *The Catcher in the Rye* whilst in Enkadar – you could go to prison for life!

These laws, stupid and facile, became more important to these teens than real life – Real World – laws.

**

"It's time to teach these bullies a lesson. Enough is enough."

There was a suspenseful silence. The Empress was possessed by fury and righteousness. Something exciting was about to happen…

Then:

"Oh great leader," Naima said eagerly. "How can we possibly fight all the bullies?"

The others looked at Naima, feeling a mixture of pity and regret. She always asked these silly questions, and it was becoming frustrating. Betty, who was supposed to be meeting her sister, didn't have time to wait for Naima to ask dozens of questions.

The Endless Empress, however, was endlessly benevolent to her followers. She smiled kindly at Naima, and responded as a mother to her daughter:

"We're going to summon the E.L.F. to aid us in our time of need."

"E.L.F.?" Truman exclaimed. He was already trying to find words to rhyme with elf.

"The Enkadarian Liberation Front," Portia explained patiently. "All countries have a secret service to protect them. The E.L.F. is ours!"

"Bullies beware!" Naima called out triumphantly.

Portia was delighted by Naima's enthusiastic support for her latest pet project.

"I'm glad someone understands why E.L.F. is so important!"

Captain Quirk piped up: "Can't we think of a better name?"

***

"We used to have such fun in Truman's attic…" Carly said as the surly waitress brought over a fresh pot of tea. The place was noisy, and the reek of burnt toast and fried food wafted out of the small kitchen. Molly hated it with a powerful passion.

Carly didn't notice Molly rolling her eyes derisively. Molly really didn't have the time – or inclination – to endure Carly's lapses in memory. But Molly quickly (and often) reminded herself why she was really doing this interview. *I'll get what I want if I stick with Carly,* Molly thought ferociously. *And I want the Endless Empress.*

***

"We will dirty our feet on the streets of Milordahl so we can punish one of these bullies," The Empress declared. "But which one shall it be?"

The Citizens of Enkadar held aloft notepads, all of which Beehive Betty had pinched off her older sister. They patiently looked at the faces. Then they jotted notes about which one of the faces deserved to be punched.

One face – a slightly sallow youth with bushy eyebrows – infuriated Beehive Betty.

"Robbie Bissett is a right scumbag," she instantly declared. "He threw my wig in the bin last week when Mr Blackmore went to see the Headmaster. I hate him."

"A deserving candidate for our plans," The Empress nodded serenely.

"Boys can be so mean," Naima whispered sadly.

But Truman Crapote had another candidate in mind.

The others watched as he tore one of the photographs off the wall in a slightly fey frenzy, and then waved it at them, his voice rising to a high pitch:

"Gary Markham must be our target!" Truman squealed. "He is utterly black-hearted. He also broke one of our most sacred laws."

"Which law did he break?" Commander Carly asked casually.

"He was so unbelievably horrible to me," Truman wailed.

"But which law did he break?!" Carly repeated.

"He told me I needed to take some poetry lessons. Doesn't that contravene Law number eighty-seven? *We Shall Not Insult Truman's Poetry.*"

An uncomfortable silence filled the Embassy. Why? Because Gary Markham was right: Truman was an unbelievably bad poet.

"I think we should hear the other nominations," The Empress stated tersely.

"I don't remember that being one of our laws," Naima whispered into Commander Carly's left ear, but Carly merely shrugged. She had broken that law many, many times in the past. And she would probably break it again at some point soon.

***

"We made a pact to do whatever it took to defend Enkadar from bullies," Carly said as Molly listened intently.

"And what did you do?"

Carly thought about it, and then she replied:

"We accidentally killed someone."

Molly, without meaning to, had just stumbled across an unsolved murder.

WE HATE IT WHEN OUR FRIENDS BECOME MURDERERS...OR WORSE, BUS DRIVERS

The Hunt for the Endless Empress

Naima looked up at her front door with a sense of weariness. One week had passed since The Empress had tricked her into leaving the flat. One week since Kai had left her for someone blonder and uglier. Naima had become the one thing she had never thought she would become: she was officially a single parent.

As she sat in silence inside her rotten old flat, a roll of wallpaper slipped off the hall wall and plopped onto the lino. Naima would have burst into tears at the injustice of everything but she had no grief inside her – only rage. She had lost everything and there was only one person she could blame: Portia Penelope Pinkerton. The hideous Endless Empress! In Naima's muddled mind, Portia had built her up and dragged her down when everything went wrong. None of the fault lay with her rotten ex-boyfriend; no, it was Portia all the way.

But how could Naima teach Portia the lesson she richly deserved? How could she finally strike out and destroy her once and for all?

The police were already after Portia and yet she continued to elude them. Every police force in the country was on standby: The Endless Empress was an automatic red alert – a status given only to the worst terrorists. A dubious honour when Naima considered that Portia was still a teenager. Naima toyed with the idea of confessing all to the police, but she'd already escaped a jail sentence for the murder of over one thousand people. Besides, the murders were really Portia's fault, just like everything else rotten in Naima's life.

Naima wasn't surprised when her telephone trilled noisily in the background.

"Speak of the devil and she's sure to call," Naima said icily.

"Oh darling," Portia said on the other side, *"I'm not the devil. I'm an activist fighting against unbelievers, oppressors and bus drivers."*

***

Portia had a real grudge against bus drivers due to a bad past experience. Bus drivers made her physically sick! She once kicked a bus driver to death in her most expensive heels, a few days after her fifteenth birthday. She got so mad for staining those heels that she continued kicking his corpse into a pulp! The poor man had made the mistake of stopping his bus and offering Portia a ride. Portia got very angry when the driver informed her that 'Enkadar wasn't on the route,' and she reacted violently. The toasted remains of the bus were found a few days later along with the driver's battered body. This was two years after The Masterpiece, but Naima recognised Portia's handiwork when the story broke on the national news. Leaving ripped-out pages from *Catcher in the Rye* beside the body was quite a give-away.

***

"What do you want now?" Naima grumbled. "Haven't you done enough damage?"

"*Hah!*" Portia cackled. "*I'm only just getting started!*"

"And I'm turning off my phone!" Naima yelled. In the background her baby started crying. *Damn*, Naima thought, *I'm all out of SleepEazy.*

"*Don't hang up!*" Portia's voice was uncharacteristically panic stricken.

"Why?" Naima demanded, enjoying her brief moment of power.

"*Because...*" The Empress said uneasily, "*...I need your help.*"

Naima nearly dropped the telephone in astonishment. Instead, she found herself asking:

"What do you want me to do?"

EXERCISE CAN KILL YOU

The glorious and great nation of Enkadar was at war! After years of simmering tensions between Enkadar and the Real World, war was finally declared against the people of Milordahl. But who would be the first target?

Who did the Citizens select from the photographs on the wall?

They debated and deliberated until the vote became unanimous.

Then, after the vote had been cast, The Empress changed her mind and selected a completely different target who wasn't even on the wall. Regardless, the gang spent days holed up in Truman's attic, plotting ways of taking revenge on the bully.

But somewhere along the way, the word 'bully' became 'unbeliever', and the word 'revenge' became 'justice'.

***

Captain Quirk watched in fascination as The Empress brewed up a strange concoction in her kitchen. He was nervous but excited at the prospect of what was to come. He examined the array of bottles stacked up along the worktop beside the gigantic chrome-plated cooker: bleach, paint-stripper, pepper, Fairy liquid, charcoal, sherbet, writhing worms and fun gummy candy. Hobs were hot, pots bubbled away, smells drifted lazily and the acid tang in the air made Quirk's eyes tingle with tears.

It looked as if a witch had commandeered the Pinkerton family kitchen.

"What are you doing?" Captain Quirk asked carefully.

"I'm mixing a magick potion," The Endless Empress replied as she emptied a bottle of industrial-strength bleach into the nearest pot. "Do you know that we of Enkadar invented many items you take for granted. We invented the paint brush, the television set, the internet – and we also invented chocolate." .

Her voice suddenly hardened. "But the Real World stole these things from us and claimed credit!"

Dials were adjusted with the skill of a master chef. Portia gave off an air of confidence in the kitchen, the manner of having made plenty of these potions in the past. And though Captain Quirk knew that Portia's real skills lay inside the Chemistry classroom, no-one dared say this to her, because she preferred being best at Art.

"I have observed the Real World for many years," Portia whispered, "and that is why I must destroy it. I don't want to be part of Milordahl, darling."

Captain Quirk's mind wandered away into his own private Enkadar.

Her Holiness stopped, put down a pot, and asked the Captain a simple question:

"Do you believe in Enkadar or do you just *believe* that

you believe in Enkadar?"

Quirk knew he had to be careful in answering her question. He thought about his reasons for joining Enkadar: he wanted to have purpose in his life. But sometimes, in quiet moments, he felt foolish being part of it.

"Yes," he said with more conviction than he felt, "I believe in Enkadar."

They both laughed in relief.

Then Quirk looked at the seething pot and asked, "What does this stuff actually do?"

The Empress stopped stirring her pots. When she spoke again, it was in character – and she had decided to play the role of the Wicked Witch of the West.

It was an eerily accurate performance.

"It's a magickal potion, dearie," she cackled with a melodramatic wiggle of her jeweled fingers. "It vanquishes unbelievers!"

***

Their target was a boy named Darryl Meyer. Darryl, an athletic fifteen-year-old, had dumped his lunch over Portia's head a few weeks before. This wasn't an unusual occurrence: many people at school threw things at Portia. But Portia seethed about this for days afterwards. She had been drifting through a daydream when the potato salad had hit her on the face.

Every daydream after that day involved force-feeding Darryl his lunch until he burst open.

And we all know The Endless Empress has a way of making her dreams come true...

***

It was late at night, because war works best in the dark.

The E.L.F. was out on the streets, armed and (sort of) dangerous. They were together, dressed in their Enkadarian finery, looking utterly ridiculous – but drawing strength from this outrageousness. They had each other. They were invincible and The Empress wasn't yet massively homicidal.

(But the night was young and there was still plenty of time for Portia to go insane.)

"What are we waiting for?" Commander Carly asked, her breath almost crystallising in the cold. She was certain that, had her chemistry teacher been there, he would have had something profound to say about the process involved in crystallisation.

They were hiding in a gloomy alley beside the local gym. Darryl Meyer, a thug as well as an unbeliever, enjoyed his weekly kickboxing classes and never missed a session. The gym was situated beside a construction site, where houses had been being built until the company had gone bankrupt. Now the houses were permanently unfinished, broken bricked-up structures with metal scaffolding sticking out like nasty Ker-Plunk. But the shadows cast by the fragmentary houses were ideal for the E.L.F.'s night-time mission.

Truman, fearful, had warned the others of dark rumours surrounding big Darryl.

"His kickboxing teacher is a black belt, or somewhere near..."

"Yes?" Naima Supreme asked cautiously.

"And even he cowers from Darryl Meyer in fear!"

Betty laughed at Truman's compulsive rhyming, but the others didn't join her.

"I hate you so very much," she told Truman. She wasn't lying.

Someone was walking across the car park. He was large and wore a tracksuit top exactly like Darryl's typical black and white hoodie.

"I think that's him!" Commander Carly hissed.

They had been waiting all night for Darryl to leave his kickboxing class, and they were tense with anticipation. Each Citizen of Enkadar had brought a weapon with them, and their respective weapons fitted their colourful personalities:

Commander Carly raised her tennis racket, a gift left to her in her grandmother's will. Beehive Betty held aloft her yo-yo, which she could swing with expert precision. No trick was beyond her! She could walk the dog, go around the world, and hit a big bully on the head. She had wanted to use her hairspray, but the yo-yo looked quirkier. Truman clutched his thesaurus, a book so hefty that it hurt his arms to carry it around. Captain Quirk had his trusty boxing gloves, an unwelcome reminder of his training sessions…but the only true weapon he could land his hands on at short notice.

And The Empress was armed with two water pistols, both of which dripped with venom. But they weren't the only weapons at her disposal. Because it was so dark, the others hadn't noticed Her Holiness crouching down and picking something up from the ground. It was heavy and rough and sat snugly in the palm of her left hand.

Portia had discovered the remains of a very large brick.

But the others knew nothing of this and Portia intended to keep it that way until…

"Unbelievers beware!" Naima squeaked with excitement.

"We're going to give Darryl a scare," Beehive Betty added while looking at Truman.

Truman frowned. Someone had just beaten him to an easy rhyme.

"Oh yes," The Empress whispered. "I promise you all he'll be scared."

They watched Darryl stop, as though he felt their presence.

But he had only stopped to adjust his headphones.

He wouldn't even hear the gang until it was far too late.

***

Without uttering another word, The Empress ran right at Darryl – and when she drew close enough she raised her left hand in a perfect circular arc.

The others still didn't realise she had a brick in her hand. From where they stood, it looked as if Portia had punched Darryl on the back of his head.

"Unbelievers must be purged!" Commander Carly yelled as Darryl staggered.

That's when the others joined in the attack.

Darryl was startled by the ferocity of the surprise assault, and his face was already streaked with blood. He didn't even get a chance to defend himself.

The Citizens of Enkadar knew Darryl was a capable fighter, so their tactic had been to take him by surprise. They weren't going to hurt him badly, just give him a little scare. Poor Darryl recoiled as a yo-yo clonked him on the skull. He stumbled as Captain Quirk's gloved hands dealt some much-needed punishment. Commander Carly laughed as her tennis racquet felled him to his knees. Truman, sadly, didn't get a chance to hit him with his thesaurus. Why? Because he was too puny to raise it above his head!

Darryl rolled around on the ground, crying for his parents. It was a horrible sound, and for a flash of a second…Commander Carly felt agonising sympathy for him.

"Take a message back to your overlords in Milordahl," The Empress announced as she raised her water pistols at

Darryl's face. "Our world is as real as your world, and our citizens deserve respect."

She fired the pistols at his face and he screamed as it burned.

"Don't bother telling the police what happened here tonight," The Empress hissed at the squealing boy. She punctuated every second word with a kick. "We have an ironclad alibi and no-one will believe you anyway!"

***

The Endless Empress wasn't lying to Darryl. The gang did indeed have an alibi. Their alibi sat in front of a television whilst they carried out their attack. She blinked unthinkingly, an automatic function of her body, but the eyes beneath the lids didn't see anything. The little tartan quilt wrapped around the old woman was adequate for the room temperature. Sitting beside her on a dusty little table was a china saucer; fruit shortcake from last week was scattered on the plate. Fruit shortcake had been her favourite treat until Alzheimer's had made her question even the littlest things in life.

Old Mrs Stanza was surrounded by shop-window dummies dressed as her son and his friends. Every now and then she spoke to them…and in her splintered recollection they spoke back. They were good to her, and she enjoyed their company.

Darryl Meyer stopped screaming and lay deathly still on the pavement.

The Citizens of Enkadar felt amazing. They had seized their destinies and struck out at the evil bullies. By bullying a bully, they were showing everyone they weren't going to be bullied anymore. This was a truly important moment in Enkadar's history.

The teens danced happily around the lifeless body of Darryl Meyer, celebrating their supreme success. They sang the Enkadarian national anthem. It stunk.

They were still dancing when Naima spotted Darryl Meyer at the opposite end of the street, his arm around a girl.

That's when they all realised that whoever they'd just battered…it wasn't Darryl.

They had got the wrong boy.

***

"We killed him!" Captain Quirk wept as they ran home. "We killed him."

"We killed *someone*," Beehive Betty added, but said nothing more.

"I broke my tennis racquet," Commander Carly kept repeating. It was snapped in half, hanging by a bit of plastic thread. She couldn't comprehend the enormity of her crime, so she focussed instead on her racquet.

"We'll be arrested!" Truman whispered. He was numb with shock.

"No," The Empress vowed with absolute certainty. "No, we won't."

***

And she was right.

THE DESOLATION OF SMUG
The Hunt for the Endless Empress

Naima left Princess with a neighbour and waited outside for a car to pick her up. She had been assured by The Empress that a car would arrive, and then she would be taken to a secret location. She was also told NOT to tell the police. Naima didn't particularly want to help her old friend, but she also couldn't refuse and Portia knew it. The secrets that forced the Citizens of Enkadar to hate each other also kept them united in a unique bond.

An ice-cream van toddled up the street and stopped outside Naima's flat.

Elvis was at the steering wheel.

"No," Naima whined, "I don't want to go inside *that*! Can't I get a taxi instead?"

The happy jingle of the ice-cream van started off nicely, but soon became a sinister twisted thing. Naima quickly entered the brightly-coloured van and prayed the jingle wouldn't awaken her baby. It had taken twenty minutes to get her to sleep!

Naima would rather take her chances with Elvis.

***

"Where are we going?" Naima asked Elvis.

The ice-cream van zoomed down streets and dark

alleys, twisting along roads until they became dirty lanes, and the houses became old factories.

"You're going to the place where Her Holiness was born."

This response brought a gasp of surprise from Naima's cracked lips:

She had heard the story, or a version of it.

And she knew exactly where she was being taken.

But what did The Empress want with her?

***

The factories used to refine oil, but now they fell apart slowly, crumbling through disuse, victims of depression. The sound of a happy ice-cream van jingle didn't belong in the air around them.

But this was what Her Holiness wanted, and Naima was curious to know why she needed help.

Naima also badly needed some gear. She was beginning to feel unwell. Sometimes, when she suffered from gear withdrawal…it felt like she was boiling alive, then when she wrapped herself up in sheets, she felt icy cold. Her nose didn't stop running, and the open windows brought in the horrors of the outside world. The noise was constantly deafening. Lack of gear made the world brighter and nastier.

***

The ice-cream van came to a grinding halt. Elvis said nothing, but Naima knew this was her final destination. She carefully climbed out of the van, dropping onto the gravel.

"I can't see Portia," Naima whispered. "Where is she hiding?"

But the ice-cream van was already reversing away from the factory.

Naima was all alone.

She didn't know what to do, so she ventured deeper into the guts of the industrial wasteland. It was cold, or maybe the gear made her feel cold, but Naima shivered a lot. She found herself moving through the remains of an office which had no roof on it. She emerged from the other side to find old cracked pipes.

Something fluttered past Naima's face, carried by a gust of wind. She screamed in involuntary fear, then laughed when she realised it was just a bit of litter.

But it wasn't litter.

It was the torn page of a book.

Naima found several more pages of the book, and she followed them like a treasure trail. The pages had been torn from a collection of fairy tales. She looked at the top of one scrunched-up page to see a title: HANSEL AND GRETEL.

Another page had been violently torn from LITTLE RED RIDING HOOD.

"She's definitely been here," Naima said to the wind.

Naima followed the pages until…

She heard a telephone ringing faintly in the near distance.

The muffled sound came from a large rusty locker.

"Do I really want to open this up?" she asked herself.

She opened it up nonetheless and peered inside the dusty gloom.

There was a mobile telephone sitting on top of something furry.

Naima reached down for the phone,

And a claw reached out of the darkness and wrapped itself around her forearm.

Naima pulled away and screamed.

The claw's owner came into the light.

The face was battered and bruised, but Naima recognised it immediately.

It was Kai, her boyfriend!

Dressed as the Big Bad Wolf.

***

Naima felt the telephone vibrate in her hand, so she put it to her ear and listened.

"I don't understand…" she sniffed miserably.

The voice on the other end was muffled, but it was undeniably Portia.

"*You're weak,*" she hissed. "*You let them win.*"

"You damn cow," Naima protested, "I don't know what

you're talking about!"

"You let them win!" Portia repeated in an accusatory voice. *"The evil forces of Milordahl! You let yourself slip back into the Real World. It didn't take long for you to lose your imagination. But don't worry...everything will be okay...I've returned to rescue you from their prison camp."*

"I don't need to be rescued," Naima said unconvincingly.

The Empress ignored Naima completely.

"The war is about to begin again...if you don't return...I can't protect you..."

"I can't go back to your land of merry make-believe," Naima replied, her voice straining in exasperation. But at least this confirmed (in her mind) her earlier suspicion – that Portia had placed that reunion advert in the newspaper.

"Portia..."

"I'm no longer that girl. She is gone. I am The Endless Empress. I am forever."

"Portia!"

"Since the day I was locked away...I am forever...I became the dark and it became me."

Naima's eyes darted towards the locker where her boyfriend currently lay. Could this be the actual locker The Bookworm had used to trap Portia when she was a little girl? Naima frowned, because she had never quite believed that story.

"You said you wanted me to help you! What do you want me to do?"

"*I want you to take out the trash,*" The Empress said reasonably.

Then Naima saw the knife sitting at the foot of the locker. It was large and nasty. What was it doing abandoned beside Kai's feet?

Naima leaned down and picked it up.

Kai, gagged as well as bound with rope, reacted badly. He wriggled a little bit more, which was about all he could do inside the locker.

"*I want you to use that knife on the scumbag inside the locker!*" The Empress begged.

"*Kill him and come back home!*"

Naima examined the knife. She saw a mental image of Kai in the shopping centre, his arms wrapped around that other girl, kissing her like he didn't kiss Naima.

"*What can he offer the Real World anyway? We won't lose much when he dies.*"

"My daughter will lose her father!" Naima croaked indignantly.

"*He has a daughter with his other girlfriend, Naima. You do know that, don't you?*"

Fury spurred Naima into action. She raised the knife above her head.

The knife flickered down!

And then…

THE WARFARE STATE

The doctors knew Carly was making a full recovery when she started ordering three-course meals from the hospital kitchen. It would only be a matter of time before they could sign the papers and set her free.

And freedom was what Carly wanted, because freedom meant she could take revenge on her oldest friend.

The nurses were even allowing her to go to the toilet on her own.

Well, *some* of the nurses...

***

"I assure you I won't be throwing up my dinner tonight," Carly said testily.

"We can't take that chance," the Nurse at the foot of the bed replied, with a smirk on her heavily made-up face. The pockets of her uniform, Carly noted, were yet again crammed full of potatoes and butter. The Nurse loathed Carly, and hid this fact as well as she hid her pocket potatoes. She only got away with treating people badly because of her grubby white uniform, which automatically made everyone believe she knew what she was really doing.

She didn't.

"I am going to the toilet and I'm going alone!" Carly yelled, not unreasonably. "I really do feel much better."

The Nurse arched an eyebrow, before moving away from the hospital bed without a further word. Carly smiled proudly and made her way to the nearest toilet.

***

Carly was washing her hands in the sink, but staring at the mirror. It was a grubby little lavatory. The cleaners didn't do their jobs properly. How the hospital hadn't been shut down was something Carly couldn't understand.

It certainly wasn't up to *her* standards!

A lone toilet flushed away in the background. Carly watched her face twist into a little frown in the mirror opposite; she'd had no idea another cubicle was occupied.

The cubicle door opened and a nurse stepped out. She moved over towards Carly and the sink. The nurse smiled brightly as she washed her hands, though not in the requisite germ-eliminating manner, Carly realised.

Carly felt a genuine sense of annoyance. The nurses really had no trust in her! They'd actually sent one of their agents to spy on her – to see if she really did digest her food. Carly looked at the nurse and prepared a verbal barrage against her.

The words withered inside Carly's throat.

There, standing in front of her, was the Endless Empress.

In a nurse's uniform!

"Is this a fantasy or are you real?" Carly cried out.

"Darling," The Empress said dubiously, "I assure you I'm quite real and alive."

"Did you stick around to see the explosion?" Carly asked, her voice trembling.

"Yessssss," The Empress sighed, eyes shut. "I felt the heat of the fire and heard the screams. I needed to use moisturiser for days and days afterwards. The explosion rocked the Real World and reverberated into Enkadar. We celebrated with parades and parties and lots of food! I ate for days and danced with unicorns."

Carly felt her own sort of explosion. It came from anger deep inside:

"THIS ISN'T ONE OF YOUR CRAZY FANTASIES!"

The Empress reacted badly; she was visibly upset, with an expression like a crushed trifle. Carly had done something unforgiveable – she had pulled Portia out of Enkadar, and landed her smack back in the Real World.

There could only be one punishment suitable for Carly's impertinence.

"You fat cow," Portia snarled, landing a verbal punch where it hit hardest. "You are small-minded, but that's the only thing that's small about you!"

"You taught me that I can be whatever I want!"

"You should be on your knees begging me to forgive you!"

Carly covered her ears and sang a merry tune –

anything to block out the rants.

Portia yelled more insults, and showed off the cigarette burns on her arms.

Carly pulled her fingers out of her ears, and laughed:

"Can we just fight and finish this off?"

***

The Empress charged across the lavatory and slapped Carly on the face. Carly blocked the second attack and landed a punch in Portia's gut with her free hand. She managed to tear some of Portia's fake nurse's uniform, exposing fabric underneath. The two girls scrapped in the restroom until The Empress emerged victorious. She seized Carly and violently yanked her hair until screams could be heard everywhere. Carly had no chance. The Empress possessed the strength of the insane, and she was confident in her power.

"Did you honestly think you could beat me?" The Empress hissed in Carly's ear.

Carly mumbled something vague. She felt like her teeth were broken. Pain speared her body – a result of being bashed against a ceramic sink over and over again.

"I'm The Endless Empress, and you're the crap I've just stepped on!"

Carly gasped some swear words at the Empress.

The Empress smashed her head down on the hard floor once, twice, three times.

Then she dragged Carly to the nearest toilet and flushed her head down it. The water swirled fast, and Carly choked on it. Then there was the awful smell. It was foul, pungent and sickening. Carly threw up. She was used to throwing up.

"There is a journalist trying to track me down. She calls herself Molly McCrumb, but that is not her real name. You are to ignore any attempts at contact. She is to be completely disregarded. Do you understand, darling?"

Carly's thoughts were groggy, but she repeated the name like a silent prayer, over and over again. Molly McCrumb. She *had* to contact this mysterious journalist. Molly McCrumb. What was it about her that was rattling Portia so much? Molly McCrumb. Why is Portia so afraid of being tracked down by her? Molly McCrumb. Carly instinctively knew she had the means to take revenge on The Empress. Molly McCrumb. Molly McCrumb. Molly McCrumb. Molly McCrumb. Molly McCrumb. Molly McCrumb.

Then Carly collapsed on the floor of the hospital toilet. Her body shut down temporarily, so it could mend itself. Maybe that was the reason she blacked out – or maybe it was because she couldn't take any more of Portia's malicious laughter...

***

When Carly awoke, she couldn't raise her head; it had

suddenly become too heavy a burden for her neck. She looked down at the floor and quickly realised it was absolutely disgusting, as if it hadn't seen disinfectant since the seventies! What was going on with the cleaners of the hospital? It was gross.

Carly's initial thought was to leave the toilet and lodge an official complaint.

Carly's second thought, however, was far more important.

It was a name. A mantra. And a prayer.

It was to be her weapon.

"Molly McCrumb!"

THE LIBERATION OF NAIMA

The Hunt for the Endless Empress

The knife swished and black tape snapped under the pressure of the blade.

"Come on!" Naima cried out. "We've got to get out of here!"

But Kai had other plans – and none of them involved the mother of his daughter.

He stood up and desperately pulled at his wolf costume, terrified any of his friends might see him dressed up in a stupid outfit. But he couldn't unzip the costume, because his hands were trembling so hard.

"What the hell are you doing? Don't let him escape. Make him pay for what he did to you!"

Naima looked down at the phone in her hand, and then she looked at Kai.

The Big Bad Wolf was running in the opposite direction.

"I can see you," The Empress cackled. *"You're eating your boyfriend's dust."*

Naima dropped the phone on the concrete, but kept the knife firmly in her other hand. She called over for Kai to stop running, but he didn't stop. She wouldn't hurt him. She could never hurt him. So why was he running away?

"Kai!" she yelled. "Come back!"

But he didn't come back.

Naima chased him and didn't stop running until he

stopped. His wolf paws didn't support his ankles, not as well as his bright white Nike shoes he never took off.

Kai fell, and quickly got back up. His face was pinky blue with rage.

Then he was in Naima's face, shouting hotly:

"This is your fault! I don't love you. I hate you! Leave me alone!"

Naima stood absolutely still, knife in hand, and said nothing. She didn't actually know how she was feeling at that moment in time. It took her a few seconds to process the sensations; fear, hope, worry, love and finally… deliverance.

***

A few seconds passed before Naima looked down on the Big Bad Wolf's body; his furry costume now a body bag on the grass. He burped a big bubble of blood, which burst between his lips. Some of it hit Naima on the face; the rest of the spray was carried away as he crumpled to the ground.

Naima casually dropped the knife onto the grass and walked away from the factory.

The police would blame The Endless Empress for this latest horrible murder.

Again.

I WAS A TEENAGE POETRY ASSASSIN

The careers advisor at Castlekrankie High School didn't seem to take Truman Crapote seriously. But quite frankly, who did?

"What do you want to do with your life when you leave school?"

Truman answered without hesitation:

"I want to write life-affirming poetry of unbounded glory!"

Truman's advisor took a deep steadying breath and asked:

"What *else* do you want to do?"

The advisor had barely survived Truman's latest collection of poetry. She didn't want to be responsible for unleashing his dubious talents on the world. Best nip this one in the bud before it spiraled out of control.

"Well," Truman whispered painfully. "I'm good at rewiring and electronic engineering."

***

It wasn't a lie. Truman was extremely good with electronics. He learned from a young age to fix things around his house, because his mother wasn't capable of doing it. Truman's mother had grown to be forgetful in her old age. Truman hadn't come to her at a young age, and she openly blamed him for sucking all the goodness out of her body. An extremely late pregnancy, Truman's mother decided to keep him because she knew it wouldn't be long before he had to keep her. Having a son would be much cheaper than hiring full-time care. The onset of dementia robbed Elspeth Stanza of her powerful mental faculties, leaving her with confusion and an extremely bitter son.

But Truman possessed the gift of poetry.

It's a shame he couldn't find the receipts.

***

Truman wept bitterly on his 13th birthday for everything he had and all the things he lacked. His new friend Portia Penelope Pinkerton was on hand to soothe his troubled mind. She was his equal, a visionary who could see into other worlds, and bring people into those worlds. He hadn't met anyone quite like Portia. He couldn't imagine his life without her kindly encouragement.

And right now, he needed that more than ever.

"What do I have to look forward to?" he said through the wreckage of an old silk handkerchief that had once belonged to his grandmother. He used it to blow his nose because it made him look somewhat pretentious. Truman was not the sort to use toilet roll to blow his nose!

"I'll be looking after that senile dingbat my entire life," he sobbed melodramatically. "I can't take the strife!"

"I'll help you look after her," Portia, not quite Empress of Enkadar, said cutely.

"What's the point?" Truman replied without rhyme, as he did when things were serious. "I'll have to spend my life working in a crappy factory, paying taxes until I lose the ability to write poetry! I might as well be dead."

Portia smiled mysteriously.

She leaned forward and kissed Truman on the nose, then said quietly:

"We don't pay taxes in Enkadar."

***

"Do you actually shop here every week?" Portia asked Truman with a slightly haughty tone. The two teenagers shared an intense friendship, but Portia's outright snobbery sometimes irked Truman. But Truman valued Portia's friendship regardless. Portia would sometimes escort him to the Castlekrankie branch of Planet Pound, where he did his grocery shopping; his mother was too feeble to leave the house let alone push a trolley full of rations. It was part of her friendship duties.

"You should think before you speak," Truman replied with sharpness in his voice. "You know fine well I shop here every week. I've started writing a ballad about this supermarket. It's a twenty-verse song. Do you want to hear it?"

"NO!" Portia shrieked in fear, before realising her reaction had been a bit too blunt. "I mean – no, I'll hear it later. A fine verse can't be fully appreciated when recited in a budget supermarket. Perform it at the Embassy where I can…appreciate it better."

Goodness, Portia thought rebelliously, *I nearly had to listen to one of his poems!*

Listening to Truman's poems was <u>not</u> part of her friendship duties.

***

It was always embarrassing when Truman's mobile telephone went off during lessons. He had to go to school, so he couldn't always be at home with his mother, but at the same time he couldn't completely abandon her to her dementia. So he kept in constant contact with her. Constant contact meant constantly having his phone next to him. It could go off at any time and he would have to answer it.

Sometimes, if it were a particularly bad day, his little Union Jack telephone would ring every ten seconds: *I'm In The Mood For Dancing* by The Nolans was the ringtone of dementia. But it was worse than mere forgetfulness; the phone bills at home were damaging to the weekly shopping budget. A few seconds after putting the phone back on the receiver, Elspeth would genuinely forget she'd just phoned her son!

***

The classroom came alive during English lessons to the sound of The Nolans. Everyone started laughing at Truman's indignity. The future Poet Laureate of Enkadar burned with embarrassment. He fished out the little phone with a cracked red, white and blue flag plastic container around it.

"Where's the damn flour?!" a woman's voice shrieked.

Truman sighed. His mother was trying to bake cakes again.

Please turn off the cooker when you're done, Truman thought frantically.

"The flour is in the cluttered cupboard beside the custard," he replied.

"Thank you my little sugar pudding soldier!"

Elspeth Stanza slammed the phone down, and presumably went back to baking cakes for her son. No-one else came to the house other than his friends.

Truman looked around his classroom at all the different faces, little knowing they'd all be gone in less than a year – every single one obliterated by fire. He smiled meekly, accepting that nothing could be done about what they had just witnessed.

The Nolans started singing again and Truman felt himself becoming violently nervous.

Solara Jones, a face on the wall in Truman's attic, finally lost her patience. This was, after all, the eighth time Elspeth had called her son during the lesson.

"This is getting ridiculous!" Solara cried out indignantly to the teacher.

Truman put the phone to his ear and waited for the inevitable question:

"Where's the damn flour?!"

"The flour is in the cluttered cupboard beside the custard," Truman sighed.

"Thank you my little sugar pudding soldier!"

***

Years after The Masterpiece and trial, Truman was startled to find a message on his answering machine when he arrived home from Planet Pound. This was very strange! Death threats from the locals had forced him ex-directory, so his telephone number wasn't widely known. Truman dropped his groceries on the threadbare hall carpet and viciously jabbed the PLAY button.

"Hello," a little voice said before it collected itself, *"my name is Molly McCrumb and I'm a journalist. Please hear me out before you delete this message!"*

There was something about the voice. It pricked Truman's memory.

The voice, smoothly professional, started again but Truman still couldn't quite place it:

"*I'm planning on writing a feature about The Masterpiece in time for the anniversary. I would love to interview you and get your side of the story. I know things haven't been easy for you over the years. This is a chance for you to let it all go once and for all! Does that sound good? I'm not a bitch or a backstabber.*" (Molly actually said that without laughing.) "*I'll write the truth. And...*"

Truman waited. He sensed the journalist wasn't quite telling the truth.

"*...If you have any information about The Endless Empress then I hope you can tell me. I'll treat you as a fully protected source. I don't believe she's dead.*"

The journalist left a telephone number and an email address.

Truman deleted the message and headed into his kitchen.

***

Flour was scattered across the floor and worktops.

DON'T ACCIDENTALLY RECORD VOICES IN A CAFÉ FULL OF ANNOYING PEOPLE, OKAY?

The Hunt for the Endless Empress

PLEASINGLY PLUMP CAFÉ PATRON:
Can I have another helping of slab cake and custard?
**BLONDE WAITRESS WITH A TIARA
AND AN ATTITUDE PROBLEM:**
Another helping? You've already had three. Don't you want a sandwich instead?
PLEASINGLY PLUMP CAFÉ PATRON:
(*obviously hurt by the stinging tone of the Waitress's voice*):
No, I don't want a sandwich. I want more of your delicious slab cake and custard. I'm a paying customer here and if I want something to eat then it is your duty to get me what I want!
**BOHO CHIC STUDENT WITH
SHOULDERS LIKE HULK HOGAN:**
Excuse me but I ordered a cup of coffee ten minutes ago.
**BLONDE WAITRESS WITH A TIARA
AND AN ATTITUDE PROBLEM:**
So?
**BOHO CHIC STUDENT WITH
SHOULDERS LIKE HULK HOGAN:**
Well…it doesn't take ten minutes to boil a kettle!

**BLONDE WAITRESS WITH A TIARA
AND AN ATTITUDE PROBLEM:**
You haven't seen our kettle! It belongs in a museum,
not a kitchen.
**BOHO CHIC STUDENT WITH
SHOULDERS LIKE HULK HOGAN:**
I need a coffee.
PLEASINGLY PLUMP CAFÉ PATRON:
I've changed my mind. I'll have a sandwich.
**UNTRUSTWORTHY JOURNALIST
WITH A DARK SECRET:**
This café is absolute mayhem!

***

"Could you please say that again?" Carly asked. "It's a bit
loud in here!"

Molly sighed theatrically and repeated what she had
just said to Carly:

"This café is absolute mayhem."

The blonde waitress had just returned from her lunch
break to find the café was still mobbed with customers. The
owner of the café shrugged innocently and continued his
hard work in the kitchen – he was making sandwiches. Lots
and lots of sandwiches packed with a variety of tasty fillings
and *very* special ingredients.

THE UNICORN OF ANNIHILATION

Each and every Saturday morning without fail, the upwardly mobile Mr and Mrs Pinkerton escorted their little firebrand into town to visit the friendly Exit Counsellor. They could have used one of their three cars, but Mr Pinkerton was very conscious that his fine vehicles might be observed by a friend or neighbour. He really didn't want anyone to know his daughter was in therapy. So instead they used the peasant wagon, also known as The Bus. What should have been a twenty minute ride became a sixty minute ordeal. Why? Because pensioners with free bus passes ensured the bus had to stop at every single stop.

There were a lot of stops on the way into town.

Portia loathed these weekend trips to the Exit Counsellor. Not only did the bus-ride feel like a tour of Britain, it was also very boring. The bus-ride into town was far worse than the actual therapy session. Portia tried to turn the boredom into fuel for her imagination, but the world of Enkadar was so at odds with the Real World that Portia couldn't completely submerge on the bus. It was apt (in some perverse manner) that only on a bus could Portia not travel to Enkadar. The inane chitchat from her parents proved an irritating distraction too, so that didn't help.

The so-called deprogramming expert was a man named Dr Edwin Isosceles, who had received his doctorate from the University of the Internet. He was a hypnotist, a performer, a headshrinker, a magician, a wizard, a trickster.

And for his next trick, he promised to rescue Portia from Enkadar.

***

His eyes had little broken blood lines weaving around their pupils, and his breath reeked of asparagus. Portia breathed through her mouth so she wouldn't smell the fester, but in her already overactive imagination, she pictured inhaling particles of the vegetable. Nasty! Spit shot out of his mouth whenever he spoke, flying in random directions. His face was full of ugly detail and his teeth were textured yellow and green. This was Dr Isosceles and Portia wasn't impressed with him. She had ample opportunity to see right up his hairy nostrils. How? Because for this treatment to work, Edwin's face needed to be a few inches from her own. It needed to be close, he explained, so his hypnotist eyes could burn into Portia's eyes. His voice was terribly reasonable as he attempted to exploit the inconsistencies of the entire Enkadar fantasy.

But reasonable argument proved unsuccessful and left

Dr Isosceles with one last tactic to break Portia. He leaned down and screamed the words over and over:

"THERE IS NO SUCH PLACE AS ENKADAR!"

But Portia sat motionless in the face of her assailant's onslaught.

"THERE IS NO SUCH PLACE AS ENKADAR!"

Regrouping,

"THERE IS NO SUCH PLACE AS ENKADAR!"

Resisting,

"THERE IS NO SUCH PLACE AS ENKADAR!"

Rejoicing!

Portia felt none of his barrage (bar the spittle); instead she smiled and shook her head at his pitiful attempts at brainwashing. She was indomitable, her will too great to be broken. She stopped staring into the distance, and instead glared right into the large eyes of her weekend therapist. Then Portia dismantled his entire vocation in one sentence:

"You will never cross the border unless I allow it."

Dr Isosceles pulled away from the face and struggled for breath. He seemed to choke for a second, just a second. It was an impulsive noise, a primal response at being bested by a mere girl. He might have continued yelling for another few hours (free of charge) had Portia not jumped up and started screaming into *his* face.

"ENKADAR IS REAL!

MILORDAHL IS A LIE!

I AM FOREVER!"

***

Dr Isosceles quit his practice a few days afterwards and applied for asylum in Enkadar. His wish would eventually be granted. Dr Isosceles would prove extremely useful to Portia at deprogramming the sheep, helping to bring them into the glorious world of Enkadar.

He also brought into Enkadar his beloved collection of Elvis records.

***

Portia left the therapy session with an overwhelming sense of triumph, rejoicing in its failure. She enjoyed pitting her wits against old people, and coming out on top. Her parents were extremely upset for some reason, but that was of little importance to Portia.

She had more imperative matters to deal with at that very moment.

Portia had another appointment, but it wasn't with a therapist.

She was off to meet a friend from Enkadar.

Her parents tried matching her speed, but Portia skipped effortlessly away from them, leaving the elderly couple crying out for her to stop. She laughed merrily, as though playing a game, and skipped onwards until their cries faded into nothingness.

It took ten minutes of skipping before Portia Penelope Pinkerton met her friend from Enkadar. She was waiting for her outside the Mecca bingo, a place of phony brightness that masked desperation and destitution.

"You can come out now," Portia said in her Endless Empress voice.

That's when the unicorn clip-clopped out from the bingo car park. It had to wait at the zebra crossing, so cars could pass beyond the traffic lights. Then it moved across the road, avoiding pensioners in the queue for bingo books.

But this wasn't any old unicorn; it was the Unicorn of Annihilation, a creature from the florid fields of Equestrixis, a stormy place east of Enkadar's capital city.

"Your Holiness." The unicorn bowed its horn in respect.

"You have journeyed far from your home to reach me," The Empress said regally.

The Unicorn exhaled rainbows from its big brown nostrils.

"How go your therapy sessions, my Empress?"

The Empress rolled her eyes and smiled sorrowfully,

"My parents will never accept me the way I am."

This didn't please the Unicorn one little bit.

"Let me kill them," it neighed dispassionately.

"No," The Empress decreed. "They aren't bad people, they just don't realise they're trapped in a world of dreams. They think Enkadar is all in my imagination. They don't realise that *this* is the dream."

The Empress motioned around her, and urged her Unicorn to take in the local surroundings. The stallion snorted in disgust, because the world of Milordahl was a horrible place full of noise and buses and concrete and litter.

"We need to clean up the litter!" The unicorn turned and aimed its magick horn at the bingo hall, which was one good gust of wind away from destruction anyway.

"That won't be necessary!" The Empress snarled. "It was built over a hundred years ago. It'll burn down in a mysterious fire and the council authority will claim insurance. When we, the Citizens of Enkadar, strike…it will be at a worthy target. Not a crappy old bingo full of old women. Do I make myself clear?"

The unicorn bowed again, and switched the subject back to Portia's parents.

"If your parents won't accept you," it neighed, "then how are you going to bring the light of Enkadar to them?"

Portia felt incredible sadness weighing upon her, like an overwhelming burden on her shoulders, a load that crushed her heart. One day – and it would happen soon – she would need to leave home and forget her family forever.

"Do you ever think about what happened to you?" The unicorn asked.

It was referring to The Bookworm and the locker.

"No," The Empress replied frigidly.

***

Mr and Mrs Pinkerton eventually found their daughter outside the Mecca Bingo.

She was crying in front of a lamppost.

SADISTIC TEENS ADDICTED TO GEAR AND MURDER
The Hunt for the Endless Empress

Naima spent hours walking through wasteland: the gutted remains of shops, scattered car wreckage, limitless concrete ground, and the distant jingle of an ice-cream van – a sound that floated in and out of earshot, a taunting nursery rhyme.

Then something burst out of the horizon. It sped towards Naima, bearing down on her at an alarming rate. But it wasn't an ice-cream van.

It was the X39 bus!

Thank goodness. Naima could finally get back into town and report Kai's death.

"I need to get to the police station," Naima called out.

The bus didn't stop. It sped up.

A rush of terror and adrenaline washed through Naima.

She threw herself onto the tarmac and rolled until the bus passed by her.

Then the bus was gone.

***

It took some time, and Naima avoided every bus she passed...but she finally made it to Castlekrankie Police station. The main reception area was a basic affair with a curved beech counter, a few computers and lots of posters on the walls. Mean faces of criminals including – obviously – a dire photograph of a fourteen-year-old Portia Pinkerton. It had been there since the day she had unleashed her Masterpiece.

It was three (and a bit) years out of date.

"I NEED HELP!" Naima screamed at the top of her lungs. Her throat was dry and her voice a croak. She felt weak and sick. God, she needed gear soon – or she'd go mad!

The lonely receptionist behind the counter replied in a pleasant voice:

"You look like you've been dragged up and down a dirty old farm!"

Naima ignored the insult and stumbled to the desk, nearly falling through it. She was exhausted. She could have slept then and there, but sleep brought the past to life. Her body craved other things; things she couldn't ask for in a police station. Instead she piped up:

"The Endless Empress just murdered my fiancé!"

That was a lie within a lie. Kai had never proposed. But it sounded good.

Maybe I haven't completely left Enkadar, Naima thought.

The receptionist, whose name badge identified her as Clara, smiled kindly.

"The police are occupied with other cases."

Naima did a cartoonish double-take. She wasn't being

taken seriously.

"You need to get the police. The police need to get their guns. And I need Portia to get shot to pieces. She is pure evil."

The nice receptionist named Clara didn't stop smiling.

Things were beginning to get a bit strange. Naima craned her neck and looked past Clara, trying to catch sight of a random policeman.

But the station was completely empty, with the exception of Naima and Clara.

"Where are all the police?"

Clara raised her hand and revealed a large juicy doughnut with frosted pink icing.

"The police are occupied with other cases."

Clara bit deep into the delicate flaky icing and swallowed it whole.

"All of them? Like…every single policeman in town is out on the streets?"

"This doughnut is really quite delicious."

Naima backed away from Clara and out through the double doors. She knew there was no help for her at the station. She would have to go elsewhere for support.

And some gear too. That was important.

Naima's body ached for gear. She couldn't think properly.

Where was the nearest gear dealer?

Green gear would be lovely right now.

Naima was lost and confused.

Then she had a flash of inspiration:
It was time to visit an old friend.

***

Clara waited a few minutes until Naima was a safe distance away. Then, when she was sure it was safe to talk, she lifted up the telephone and dialed a number.

It didn't take long for someone to answer at the other end.

"She left a few minutes ago," Clara said flatly.

A voice crackled down the receiver.

Clara basked in praise and glowed with the joy of a job well done.

"Thank you!" she said tearfully. "I live only to serve."

And then,

"Praise Enkadar, your Holiness."

THE HAIRSPRAY QUEEN

Beehive Betty was bored from the day she was born. Her favourite hobby was antagonising people. She lived to create scenes. She loved to cause drama. For most of her young life she honestly thought she wanted to be an actress.

But Betty soon realised she wasn't an actress. She could never be satisfied simply parroting the words of other people. Her ego wasn't quite as large as that of The Empress, but it was there nevertheless, hidden deep beneath her black beehive wig.

No, Betty wasn't an actress. **She was a director.**

But she didn't just create and direct scenes! Betty soon discovered her real talent was directing...*influencing*... people. All it took to create compelling drama was for Betty to make the right comment at the wrong time.

Betty loved causing trouble and getting away with it. She loved playing cruel pranks on people, usually with the help of their closest friends...so she had someone to blame if it all went wrong. That's probably why she joined Enkadar. She sensed that she could make good use of her imagination...and her other, more dubious talents.

But Betty quickly learned that there were others in her life equally proficient in the art of causing a scene. One person in Betty's life was especially immune to her tricks. She was Betty's equal and had been since the day she was born.

Betty wasn't an only child. She had a sibling. A sister. Damn!

***

"Would you like a biscuit?" Betty asked innocuously.

Amanda McNab instantly sat upright in her bed. The television played away in the background, but she wasn't watching it. Amanda loved reading, but she could only read if she had background noise. Elizabeth, her little sister, wasn't background noise as much as she was background nothing. Amanda liked to pretend her sister didn't exist. She could never forgive her for being born.

"No," Amanda said, with a flick of her golden mane. "I'd rather eat shit."

"I was only trying to be polite," Betty retorted. She knew her sister flicked her blonde hair just to annoy her. Betty had never taken to her own ginger tresses.

"Oh please." Amanda dropped the book onto her lap. "You come here, offer me some biscuits, then you eat the rest of the packet...and then mum goes mad – because they're her biscuits – and you say it wasn't just you, that I ate them too. And then I get into trouble. I'm not falling for it. If you don't get out of my room, I'll jump off my bed and shove your can of hairspray down your throat."

Beehive Betty smirked, but inside she was furious. Amanda always got the better of her!

Beehive Betty wasn't like other teenagers her age. That was another reason she became a Citizen of Enkadar. She liked old things; retro clothes, vintage rock 'n' roll, outlandish hairstyles, classic movies. Her favourite band was Pink Floyd – she had actually sung a duet with Syd Barrett during the Enkadar Aid festival last year. It was amazing. She acted in a production of Romeo & Juliet with Leonardo DiCaprio at the Enkadar Theatre, and won a stack of awards for her sensitive portrayal of Juliet.

But one thing she couldn't do was get the better of her annoying sister!

And yet…blood is thicker than water, and bad blood is still blood regardless.

***

Beehive Betty was walking home from school with Portia, when a gang started kicking at their heels. The two Citizens of Enkadar had spent the last ten minutes discussing the magical moment Leonardo DiCaprio asked Betty out on a date, and then suddenly Portia screamed and fell onto the ground.

It happened without any warning. Solara Jones and her gang of Bimbots (an Enkadarian word that translates into clumsy Milordahl tongue as 'Bimbo Robots') were laughing and pushing the girls. There were too many of them! Betty and Portia were outmatched by sheer force of numbers.

One of them reached over and snatched Betty's amazing wig.

"I never knew you had ginger hair," the girl laughed at Betty.

"No! Give it back!" Betty howled. It was so unfair!

Betty had beautiful red hair, but she didn't like it. Her wig – a genuine vintage sixties beehive – helped transform her, and boosted her confidence. Her sister had taunted her about her hair for years. The beehive and hairspray were her shields.

And now her shield had been taken from her!

"You can't do this to us!" Portia seethed, her crazy ballerina outfit provoking laughter from the gang. "We have diplomatic immunity under the laws of Enkadar."

Solara, a statuesque cheerleader who used her fists instead of pom-poms, laughed at the absurdity of Portia's claims. (Incidentally, Solara ended up on the wall in Truman's attic two years later – an extra bully who had to be taught a violent lesson.)

"You're a creepy little freak," Solara told Portia.

"Why do you always wear this ratty thing on your head?" a girl asked Betty.

"I like how it looks on me," Betty mumbled, embarrassed.

The girl – whom neither Portia nor Betty recognised – opened her mouth and dribbled a thick glob of saliva onto the wig. Then she dropped it onto the grass and set about grinding it into the dirt. This drew bitchy laughter from Solara and the others.

They were still laughing when Betty's sister arrived and punched Solara in the face.

Amanda McNab, Betty's sister and arch enemy, momentarily became her sister's saviour – bad blood was *still* blood and not water.

"Give that back to my sister!" Amanda yelled as she took on the entire gang.

Portia was astonished to see one girl fight off an entire gang, but Betty's sister was completely fearless. Portia watched, deep in thought, thinking of ways to fight gangs and win, just like Amanda. She would never leave her house again without a weapon.

Betty, however, was mortified that her hated sister had come to the rescue.

She looked over at Portia, but her friend was lost in Enkadar.

***

"I never really took to Betty," Carly admitted ruefully in Go Joe's Café.

Molly was interested to hear more, because Carly had previously hinted at a personal dislike for Beehive Betty.

"Why?" she asked. "I need to know for my story."

Carly thought about it for a few seconds, before

answering: "She always made things worse. And then she died horribly. Oh well."

Molly suddenly had a strong urge to reach out and punch Carly in the face.

MESSINESS AT THE MEMORIAL

Last night Portia dreamt that she killed everybody at school.

It was a good dream.

***

The Citizens of Enkadar decided to bunk off class for a day. They weren't worried about the repercussions. After getting away with murder, there wasn't much that frightened them anymore. The effect on Portia had been the most dramatic: she was utterly self-assured, secure in her brilliance – but deeper inside her delusions.

She truly was Empress of her own world.

And The Empress decreed everyone was free from a boring day of lessons!

"Where are we going?" Beehive Betty enquired cautiously.

The Empress looked away from the Citizens, but not for long.

When she turned back, she held in her hands a tin of bright purple paint.

"We're going to brighten up the War Memorial."

Not one Citizen contradicted their Empress.

***

The War Memorial is an old stone column which has a plaque commemorating the fallen of World War One. There's an old bandstand nearby, which once hosted actual bands, but now appeals to drunks and addicts. It used to be green, until a local charity raised enough money to restore the bandstand to glorious gleaming silver – its original colour. Three wooden benches sit around the War Memorial, opposite the bandstand. And wreaths of beautiful red poppies appear every few weeks on the steps of the Memorial.

For years the caretaker of the Memorial – a seventy-year-old man named William Jackson – thought no-one else was interested in it.

But he was wrong.

The Endless Empress had plans for The Memorial...

***

"There's such beautiful stillness here," Captain Quirk said, his dark hair flapping in the breeze. He had never known such peace in the Real World. This place, with such solid silence, could have been a part of Enkadar. And here it was, just down the street from the shopping mall. Quirk realised that there was an entire world out there, a world that didn't have to be inside his head.

"My grandfather's name is probably on here

somewhere," Naima Supreme declared as she lowered the tins of paint she had been given to carry.

"My grandfather died in the war," Truman Crapote cried out excitedly. He was dandified to the extreme, wearing a bowler hat and a frock coat with a pink silk scarf.

"Oh?" Beehive Betty asked with genuine curiosity. "Did he die in battle?"

"No. He caught the flu and died on the day of the armistice."

Beehive Betty stifled powerful laughter, because she didn't want to hurt Truman's feelings; she also didn't want her beehive wig to fall off her head.

"My grandfather died of constipation," Commander Carly said flatly.

"Oh please!" Beehive Betty said, unconvinced. "You can't die from constipation."

"Yes you can!" Carly cried out. "If you don't go to the toilet – you die!"

"Did your grandfather live in Enkadar?" The Empress politely asked Carly.

Carly thought about it and said:

"No, he lived in an old folk's home."

"Ugh," The Empress gasped. "I hate old people. They're always going on and on about how much better things were back in their day. And they're always getting on the bus for free. I hereby decree that no pensioner is allowed in Enkadar!"

The others stood around waiting to see what Portia had

planned, although deep down, they already knew what she was going to do. It was too obvious to say aloud. The War Memorial and tins of paint suggested a message was about to be sent.

The Empress moved over to Naima, and lifted up a can of bright red paint.

"This place looks terribly shabby," The Empress acknowledged. "It could do with some redecorating. I think the paintwork in particular needs careful attention."

That's when she hurled the red tin of paint across the War Memorial.

"The War Memorial is bleeding," Truman said, almost poetically.

Beehive Betty squealed and lifted up a purple can, spinning around and hurling it at the War Memorial. She kept some at the bottom of the tin for the wooden benches. She tipped it over and poured it onto the seats.

A savage lust gripped the Citizens of Enkadar as everyone joined in with the vandalism. Paint, beautiful colours of the rainbow, were tipped and flicked across the Memorial and the plaque and the bandstand until they dripped with colour.

They were laughing at their DIY handiwork when someone shambled out from the bandstand, accompanied by a dog. Commander Carly noticed him first. He didn't see them, even though he stood in front of the group. But his guide dog helped him find the intruders at the Memorial.

"What are you damn kids doing?" the caretaker yelled. "Stop it!"

His guide dog – a big golden Labrador with a harness – barked at the Citizens.

"I hate old people," The Empress whispered.

"Go away!" The old caretaker motioned violently with his left hand. "Leave or I'll call the police and have you arrested!"

"We know our rights," Naima Supreme said haughtily. "You can't touch us!"

"Are you the caretaker?" The Empress asked, knowing full well he was. The old man, who wore medals on his clean black jacket, nodded his head. He wore dark spectacles, but behind them were vacant eyes. He was virtually blind.

"Yes," he cried out, but his voice had a tremor. "I am the caretaker."

"Then take care of yourself!" The Empress screamed.

The old man couldn't do anything as Portia rushed forward and shoved him violently onto the ground. He cried out in terror as he fell. Commander Carly backed away in horror, because she wanted nothing to do with this attack.

"Tell us all about how you survived the war!" Portia kicked the old man in the ribs.

The caretaker squirmed and caught Portia's ankle in a surprisingly tight grip.

"Get off me!" She screamed hysterically. "I'm not

going back to the locker!"

They all heard the comment, but only Carly truly understood it.

The others rushed over to help their Empress, but it took both Truman and Quirk's combined strength to free her from the caretaker. They didn't speak – they ran. They ran faster and longer than they would ever run in their lives. They didn't stop until the trees became the roads and the roads became the streets.

It was only when they felt safe that they started speaking again.

"I'm going to get him," The Empress vowed with fanatical fire in her eyes.

***

MOLLY: Did the caretaker die too?

CARLY: No, not at first.

MOLLY: What do you mean?

CARLY: The Empress made good on her promise eight months later.

MOLLY: What did she do to him?!

CARLY: She broke into his house and retrained his guide dog! Instead of leading the caretaker to the Memorial, the dog took him to the main road during rush hour.

MOLLY: …

CARLY: The caretaker was hit by a truck. His dog was

136

blinded, but survived.

MOLLY: The blind caretaker's guide dog went blind? That's ironic.

CARLY: His dog also lost a leg and a tail.

MOLLY: I need to put all this stuff into my notes. What was the dog's name?

CARLY: His name was Lucky.

MEETING IN THE LADIES ROOM

Naima was ready to flush the toilet when she heard someone say her name. It came from behind the cubicle door, close to the sinks. Naima knew this because she heard running water. It was a girl's voice, but not one Naima instantly recognised. Then she heard another voice replying to the girl.

Two voices.

Two girls.

And they were talking about her.

***

"Naima Calmar is so dirty," one of the girls cackled. Naima recoiled from the anonymity of the cubicle; not only because of the insult, but because when the girl said her name, she said it in a voice full of absolute disgust.

Quietly, so she didn't alert the two girls to her presence, Naima leaned forward and pressed her ear against the metal door that separated her from the school toilets. They were calling her names, saying she was dirty. Naima knew that wasn't true. She had two baths a day and wore good quality perfumes.

How could anyone call her dirty?

But cleanliness wasn't what the girls meant when they branded her 'dirty'.

"I'm sick of her stealing boyfriends from people," the girl said angrily.

Suddenly another voice joined in on the discussion; three voices, three girls.

And they all hated Naima Calmar passionately.

"I hear she's had, like, ten abortions."

"More like twenty!"

The girls laughed long and loud.

Naima covered her mouth in horror, because she didn't want to risk crying out in rage, or burst into tears of humiliation. How could they say things like that about her? Was that what *everyone* thought about her at school?

A fourth voice joined in on the hot topic.

"She's a swot! She gets really good grades from the teachers."

But voice #3 took issue with this comment:

"She probably had sex with them to get those grades!"

Loud laughter overwhelmed Naima's ears and she looked down at her feet. Tears freely flowed now. This was her reputation. And all of it was untrue!

"I hear she's hanging out with The Endless Empress and those other weirdoes."

Naima frowned, because up until that moment…she had no idea other people at school called Portia by her adopted Enkadarian title.

"If Naima tries to steal my boyfriend," said one of the girls – there were too many voices to count – "I'll kick her head in!"

"I'd join in. She thinks she's better than everyone else because she comes from money. But she's just a grubby tart."

Then the bell trilled and the voices left the toilets in order to get to their classes.

But Naima didn't bother going back to class. She sat there on the toilet seat, weeping in humiliation.

Naima was so upset that she didn't realise something important had just happened.

***

It was something that came back to her years later, long after The Masterpiece, long after The Empress disappeared like the smoke. It was one night during a dream, when Kai was snoring beside her, just before Princess was born, before the gear really took hold – it all suddenly came to Naima in a flash.

***

One of the mocking voices in the school toilet had belonged to Beehive Betty.

TWISTS, TURNS, AND CIGARETTE BURNS
The Hunt for the Endless Empress

Naima knocked on Truman's front door and waited for him to open it. She was astonished to see that the street where he lived – the familiar place of her time at high school – hadn't changed a bit. Memories rushed back to Naima, memories her gear-addled brain hadn't processed in years; tiny recollections hidden within the margins of her brain. Bad plans had been made in the attic at the top of Truman's house.

It wasn't an attic, Naima thought idly, *it was an official Embassy of Enkadar.*

The door opened before Naima had the chance to remember too much.

Truman stood in the hallway in what looked like a Victorian undertaker's suit.

"You look absolutely terrible! Has your day been that unbearable?"

Naima collapsed in an exhausted heap on Truman's doorstep.

Truman looked around and quickly bundled his old friend into the house.

***

The café was hot with body heat and Carly sat in front of me, staring into space, breaking her self-imposed silence with a few muttered comments directed at invisible friends only she could see. I found myself wishing all journalists came equipped with mind-reading wands rather than old Dictaphones and notepads. For all my savvy and experience, I still couldn't get a firm grip on the girl I'd spent the day interviewing. It was getting dark outside and I still didn't know where The Empress was hiding. That was the frustrating thing about this interview; I'd spent the day hearing about the past, all the time knowing *she* was out there somewhere. I knew how I wanted this story to end and Carly was the only one who could give me that ending.

I decided that I didn't want any more delays.

It was time to take control of the interview and force Carly's hand.

***

"I met Truman today," Molly blurted out.

Carly reacted very badly to this news.

"Where did you find that freak?" she spat venomously.

"He came to see me when I was outside getting air."

Carly seemed to be thinking deep important thoughts.

"He knew you were here?"

Molly suddenly realised she hadn't told him about Go Joe's Café.

"He said he was on his way to the Post Office..." she gasped.

The café was suddenly filled with Carly's cynical laughter:

"And he just happened to detour to this café?"

It sounded foolish when Carly said it aloud.

"How did he know where to find me?" Molly asked in bewilderment.

"And you call yourself a journalist?!" Carly guffawed.

"He took me to Portia's old house," Molly said, still in a daze.

Molly watched as more men came in for food. The place was dangerously overcrowded and – oddly enough – everyone seemed to be eating sandwiches. There was a poisonous vibe around the café, and Molly knew something wasn't right.

"Truman comes across as a bit of a lost soul."

"He doesn't have a soul," Carly jabbed back.

Sensing hostility, Molly decided to speak about Truman, prodding Carly until she cracked. This tactic worked spectacularly.

"He hasn't been the same since he left Enkadar," Molly added unhelpfully. "Being a former Citizen yourself, I thought you would sympathise with his plight."

"'Since he left Enkadar'?" Carly squealed. "Truman *never ever* left Enkadar. And he isn't a former Citizen – he *is* a Citizen. Truman Crapote is Portia's second in command. How do you think she's managed to stay hidden all this time? He's helping her. He has always helped her! Do you think she made a bomb by herself?"

Molly gasped, because she hadn't suspected a thing.

***

One of the customers at the far end of the café was chatting to the five men at his table, nibbling on his sandwich. They had been told to wait and watch. So everyone blended in by eating, because that's what people do in a café.

"This sandwich tastes funny," the customer said with a frown.

"What's the filling?" one of the other customers asked, his curiosity aroused.

"I don't know. But it was a freebie, so I grabbed it."

"We aren't supposed to be eating on duty," another customer said quietly.

***

Molly was still reeling from the new information.

"Truman knows where The Empress is hiding?" she asked for what felt like the tenth time. "I don't understand why he took me to her house? I don't get it."

Carly shrugged nonchalantly, before dropping another

surprise in her unsubtle way:

"I expect he was here to meet with The Empress. Either that or The Empress ordered him to take a detour. Perhaps she wanted Truman to lure you away from this café, so you wouldn't complete your interview with me."

Molly couldn't believe it. If what Carly was saying was true then...

HOLD ON.

WAIT A MINUTE.

"Did you just say he was *here* to meet with The Empress?"

Carly smiled smugly.

Then the trashy blonde waitress came to the table with a tray:

"Would you like a sandwich or a fresh pot of tea?"

Molly turned to tell the waitress to get lost, but her eyes stopped at her arms.

The waitress's arms had burn marks. They were faint, but undeniable.

Molly made a noise, a startled choking sound. She felt as though she were *seeing* the waitress for the first time. The trashy waitress looked slightly different to the famous school photographs, the shots that were on the front pages of every newspaper in the country. The face was thinner – but the eyes sparked with familiar malevolent intelligence, the same disdain that cameras had captured so effectively over the years.

Molly knew she wasn't dealing with a mere waitress.

"It's you!" Molly drew back in horror.

Her Holiness the Endless Empress of Enkadar bowed her head ever so slightly.

Then she brought up a yellow teapot and aimed it like a gun at Molly's face.

The Empress smiled pleasantly. "You'll eat a sandwich if it kills you."

Carly closed her eyes and blocked her ears with her fingers.

She knew fine well what was about to happen...and it was going to be violent.

THE RISE OF THE GLORIOUS AND GREAT NATION OF ENKADAR

The Hunt for the Endless Empress

The interview is a trap.

But whose trap is it?

Innocent people will die tonight.

***

Molly felt an overwhelming sense of dismay. She didn't speak, for words weren't enough to describe her depression. The crazy girl across the table had betrayed her.

"I gave you what you wanted," Carly protested quietly.

Molly thought she was on the trail of The Empress. She had genuinely believed she was going to trap Carly with words and questions. But Carly had set her own trap. The Empress didn't need to be tracked down: she was already there, serving sandwiches all day long in Go Joe's Café.

"I suppose it explains why you insisted on being interviewed in this dump."

Carly nodded her head sympathetically.

"I gave you what you wanted," she repeated. "And you wanted The Empress."

"And now I've got both of you," The Empress said evenly.

The yellow tea pot didn't waver an inch.

It was pressed firmly against Molly's forehead.

Molly's right hand slithered across the table to a spare piece of cutlery. A fork or a knife, it didn't matter. Either would do as a weapon. Molly felt a surge of bloodlust. She knew that no court in the world would send her to prison for killing The Empress. And if she couldn't kill her, Molly would take satisfaction in injuring her.

The Empress was a monster. She deserved to die.

"I'll baptise you with boiling water if you raise that knife an inch."

Molly slid her fingers away from the knife very, very, very slowly.

***

Truman escorted Naima into his living room, which looked faintly retro, a result of the old-fashioned tastes of Mrs Stanza. Truman fell onto his battered old couch, a comfortable-but-cracked black leather suite, and stared intensely. Naima didn't fail to notice an old blue baseball bat sitting idly at Truman's feet.

"You were right," Naima coughed. "The Empress is still alive and she contacted me too. She's completely crazy, Truman! She forced me to see her and then…"

Emotions besieged Naima, and as a result she found herself sobbing loudly. It wasn't insincere grief. She might have plunged the knife into his heart, but Naima was genuinely devastated by Kai's death. Once she started crying, she couldn't stop.

"She murdered Kai! I was there, Truman. She stabbed him to death!"

Truman nodded his head sadly, and for a moment it looked as though his black top hat might topple. He knew all of this, of course. But he was content to wait until Naima calmed down, so he listened (as all good friends do) to her version of events.

"She locked Kai away…and then she stabbed him and ran away!"

"How is your daughter?" Truman asked, out of the blue.

Naima stopped crying and wiped her puffy face with her grimy sleeve. She hadn't once thought about her daughter since leaving the police station. It was a strange question for Truman to ask. Something in his still expression unnerved Naima. Despite knowing Truman for years, Naima suddenly found him quite frightening.

She decided to change the subject away from her daughter.

"I'd like a drink of water," Naima said in a trembling voice.

Truman was too busy trying to think up a word that rhymed with 'slaughter' to fetch Naima a glass of water. He couldn't use the word 'daughter', because he'd already asked Naima about her daughter. But what rhyming word could he use?

Then, suddenly, he realised the answer was there all along:

"It's so obvious!" Truman exclaimed joyfully. "Slaughter rhymes with water!"

Naima was bewildered. This wasn't a new thing. It had become her default setting.

"Yes. I'd like a glass of water from the tap on the sink in your kitchen."

Truman raised and pointed his baseball bat in the direction of the kitchen:

"My kitchen is your kitchen," he said with a bright smile.

Naima got up and made her way towards the kitchen, but halted in the hallway. She crept towards the front door and experimentally tried the handle.

It didn't shift an inch.

Truman had locked the main door.

The bleep blippity bleeping of a telephone being dialed trailed out of the living room. Truman was phoning someone...but who?

***

The Empress was about to tip the contents of her tea pot over Molly when, just in the nick of time, the Sacred Mobile Telephone of Enkadar buzzed noisily inside Portia's apron. The Empress sighed in melodramatic annoyance. She couldn't even sigh without turning it into an attention-grabbing moment.

"Answer it," Carly said knowingly. "You don't want to keep Truman waiting."

Molly's eyes darted about the café. She said nothing, but observed everything. She wasn't going to be tricked again. And she soon noticed something peculiar.

The customers in the café hadn't left. They were the same customers as before.

None of them had left their tables.

Molly felt something was about to happen, something horrible.

"Come back to Enkadar," The Empress pleaded.

Carly was having none of it. She screwed her face up in disgust,

"I don't want anything to do with Enkadar!"

Portia snarled, and then drew back her arm. In a fit of fury, she launched the tea pot at Carly. But Carly was far too nimble. She threw herself onto the floor with lightning-fast reflexes and avoided the ceramic missile. The yellow pot shattered above Carly's head, causing boiling rain to fall. She was slightly sore, but safe.

Whilst The Empress was distracted, Molly took the opportunity to confront her – which had been her primary goal all along. She gripped the edge of her chair and shoved it backwards with enough force to hit Portia's legs. The sound of plastic chair scraping against the ground was ear-piercingly loud. The Empress staggered back slightly in surprise and pain. She hit the wall and uttered a cry of rage.

"You're going to join the dead teenagers of Castlekrankie High!" Portia snarled.

Molly roared at the top of her lungs and moved towards Portia.

But The Empress was fully recovered and ready to fight back. And she could fight!

Portia threw back her fist and punched Molly in the gut.

"I know how you fight!" The Empress declared. "I remember."

Molly caught her breath, snarled and swung a good left hook, but Portia countered then twisted until Molly lost her balance. That was when Carly leapt into the brawl. She started off by tossing unopened sachets of brown sauce at Portia. But this was a stupid thing to do, because brown sauce only hurts the taste buds. Carly decided to get more involved in the brawl, so she grabbed Portia's silver tiara and threw it across the room, then tore out a large clump of the royal hair for good measure.

It was at this point that the police got involved.

***

The café dramatically came to life. Each customer sitting at a table stood up and flashed shiny badges. They had been waiting for this moment all day.

"They're *all* undercover policemen?" Molly asked with

astonishment.

"Yes. All of the pigs are here in the café. They're on a stakeout," The Empress noted drily. "It's a shame we don't serve steak."

The strange lack of policemen in Castlekrankie – the mystery that had puzzled Naima earlier – had been solved. They were all in Go Joe's Café spying on The Empress. They had been tipped off by Commander Carly.

One of the policemen stepped forward and put his hand on Portia's shoulder.

"We'll take it from here," he said firmly. She flinched at his touch.

"You're a dead little piggy!" Portia remarked, as she rubbed her hands together.

***

She wasn't exaggerating. They were all dead. They just didn't realise it yet.

Every policeman started choking, and spitting out what resembled clotted green slime. The officer beside me, the man who had bravely stepped forward to arrest The Empress, was literally spewing out sparkling glittery funk, which sprayed against the window. He wasn't the only one in agony. Every policeman in the café spat and choked on greasy dust, all the colours of the rainbow. Carly and I watched as someone near us vomited red glitter, whilst another officer in close proximity spat out his insides.

I'm certain his guts were coated in a sticky purple dust. The smell was indescribably foul.

Carly stood screaming as one policeman burst into a storm of glittering blue dust.

***

"I told them not to eat the sandwiches," Carly cried out miserably.

Molly soon worked out what had happened to the police squad.

But before she could speak, another sound overtook the cacophony of screams.

It was an odd crunching noise, the sound of food being chewed into bits.

Carly and Molly turned to see Joe, the owner of the café, chomping down on a large sandwich – just as his Empress had ordered. Joe smiled a glittery smile.

"Portia's overdosed everyone with gear. She filled the sandwiches with it. She knew the police would be here… and she's slaughtered them all like…"

"Like everyone from school," Carly said simply.

The Endless Empress might have confirmed her theory.

But she was long gone.

"I ripped open her nurse's uniform while we were fighting at the hospital," Carly said, "and I saw she was wearing an apron with a badge. That's how I knew she worked at Go Joe's Café. But I think that was part of her trap. She *wanted* me to alert the police, so she could do *this* to them."

"It isn't nice when someone tricks you," Molly said pointedly.

It was at this moment that Carly put forward a special offer.

It was a proposal that Molly McCrumb: Kickass Journalist couldn't decline.

"Do you want to finish off your story?"

"Yes."

"Then follow me and we'll walk into Enkadar together."

Carly and Molly left the café together, and ran out into the night.

They didn't notice the X39 bus following them down the street.

THE HAIRSPRAY QUEEN PERFORMS THE HITS OF PINK FLOYD

Never ever assume that just because people claim to be united they can't ever be divided. It only takes one person to break up a group. It only takes one person to say something the others don't want to hear.

And sometimes...it might be more than just one person.

***

Beehive Betty was in the middle of rehearsing a guitar part with famous 60s rock star Syd Barrett when the Citizens of Enkadar walked into her dream. Betty wasn't entirely happy at the intrusion. So far she had gone through the entire Pink Floyd back catalogue, and now The Empress was standing in front of her, pulling a disdainful expression on her oval face.

"What is it?" Betty asked.

"You haven't been to Enkadar for weeks!"

Betty smiled falsely and shrugged her shoulders, pretending to be nonchalant. She realised her former friends were flanking Her Holiness, all of them with arms on hips. And they all wore the same imperious expression as Her Mad-jesty.

"Why are you avoiding us?" Commander Carly demanded.

Syd Barrett laughed and whispered something into Betty's ear.

She laughed too, enjoying the joke at Carly's expense.

"Bugger off, you psychedelic cretin!" The Empress snarled at Syd.

Syd Barrett faded out of the dream, but he had never actually been there in the first place.

"You've been distant with us," Naima Supreme whispered. "You'd rather spend time with the sister you hate than with your true sisters."

Beehive Betty adjusted her large wig and stood up off the wall. The grotty punk-rock rehearsal space departed and Betty was standing at the wall during school lunch break. She had always been there at the wall, eating her lunch, but her imagination had transformed it – and her – into a place where her favourite band practiced.

Beehive Betty had learned her full potential, and the potential of her imagination. And it was all thanks to Portia Penelope Pinkerton. But Betty was tired of Enkadar. It was no longer necessary. She had outgrown her old friends. She knew they couldn't do anything to harm her, because she knew too much. She had been there when they had attacked 'Darryl Meyer' and the caretaker.

She could easily speak out and destroy them all.

"I'm no longer a Citizen of Enkadar," Betty announced.

There was a gasp of horror from The Empress.

"You can't just leave us," Commander Carly stamped her foot.

"We made a pact," said Naima Supreme.

"That's a fact," Truman added.

"Oh shut up!" The Empress shushed Truman. She was stressing out over this high profile defection. Beehive Betty was a member of the Enkadarian Liberation Front, a speaker in the High Council, and part of lots of other organisations that existed solely in Portia's imagination. She couldn't leave! It wasn't allowed.

And no-one contradicted Her Holiness.

But Betty couldn't care less about Enkadar.

She put her two hands on Portia's chest and pushed her away.

They started fighting in the playground. They attracted a large crowd of teenagers, all of whom jeered and cheered on the two girls. Nothing livened up a boring school day quite like a girl fight.

A knife blade flashed in the sun, but no-one knew who'd brought it to school.

Someone screamed.

Captain Quirk staggered away from the crowd and slumped against the wall.

The fight stopped and everyone realised something was wrong.

***

"I've been cut," Quirk cried out hoarsely.

His hands were soaked in blood.

The crowd dispersed slowly, moving back in horror and shock.

The Empress held a knife in her hand, a knife covered in blood.

"It wasn't me," she cried out. "I didn't do it."

Naima Supreme and Commander Carly exchanged glances.

Beehive Betty saw her chance and leapt into the argument. She was a director, and this was her chance to direct her greatest piece of drama:

"You're an empress of lies!"

Her remark had the effect it was meant to have, and Captain Quirk suddenly looked at The Empress in disgust at her betrayal. It was quick, the change in his expression. He no longer trusted his Empress.

Then he looked down at his belly, which displayed a long slick blood streak.

"Someone get me an ambulance, and stop gawping at me for once in your lives!"

Truman Crapote was already dialing for help, but his fingers missed the correct numbers on the keypad. He felt sick with nervousness. The sight of blood upset his delicate, and poetic, sensibility.

"I didn't do it," The Empress cried out again.

But no-one was listening to her.

"I am your Empress, and you need to obey me!"

Then,

"Let's go to Enkadar and fight dragons!"

But The Empress was all alone in the middle of the playground. Portia hadn't felt this abandoned since the day she'd met The Bookworm; having no-one else believe in Enkadar was worse than being inside that locker. The Empress desperately looked around, checking to see if she was truly alone.

Truman and Naima stood in the periphery, their loyalty as sturdy as ever.

Carly took a few seconds longer, but she eventually joined Truman and Naima.

"We don't want to lose Quirk!" Carly exclaimed, her voice low with horror.

Beehive Betty raised an eyebrow, although the others didn't see it, because it was hidden beneath her enormous wig. Carly's openly bitchy remark had confirmed to Betty what she knew all along: Carly didn't like her in the slightest.

Naima Supreme didn't hear – or chose to ignore – Carly's attack on Betty.

She added:

"Do or say whatever it takes to keep them in Enkadar."

So with this in mind, The Empress made Quirk and Betty – her friends and countrymen – an offer she knew they couldn't resist:

"I'll take everyone out bowling tonight if you just forget this argument…"

Captain Quirk looked down at the cut on his belly in astonishment. He felt sick and weak. He could barely articulate what he felt at that moment, he was so angry.

"I'll pay for everything," The Empress added eagerly.

Beehive Betty smiled. She could feel ferocious anger radiating from Quirk. It was almost like heat, but it burned deeper and hotter, the temperature of resentment.

"Do you want to go bowling tonight, Richard?"

***

The Citizens of Enkadar didn't go bowling that night.

A SPLIT IN THE RANKS
The Hunt for the Endless Empress

Castlekrankie was constructed for safety. The theory is that you can open your front door and walk to anywhere in town without having to cross a road. Cavernous tunnels were built so children can explore their town without having to be near speeding cars.

Everything about the town of Castlekrankie is elegant and perfectly linked; everything is in its proper place and position. Nothing is ever out of arrangement.

And yet the X39 bus is never on the right route.

***

Carly and Molly felt the full force of the weather. It was an icy blast of the customary Castlekrankie cold. Molly staggered because she wasn't really dressed for this sort of low temperature. Her jacket was a slight silver trench coat, and her scarf was equally thin. But excitement coursed through her, and that brought a sense of exhilaration.

Then Molly looked back through the window of Go Joe's Café and shuddered. The place was full of bodies, and those bodies were once people with lives and families and friends and hobbies. They had woken up, dressed for work, gone to the café...and then they had all died together. Did they get a chance to say goodbye to their wives and children before work?

Molly suddenly felt untouched by the frosty weather.

"Come on!" Carly cried out. "She's getting away!"

But something more important was drawing Molly's attention from the matter in hand; her tape recorder was buried in her bag, where she'd shoved it after Portia's slaughter of the policemen. Molly thrust her hand deep into the bag's recesses, feeling her way through journalist junk until her fingers brushed against the familiar metal switch.

She pressed RECORD and suddenly felt much better.

***

CARLY: Are you waiting for Christmas? Come on!
MOLLY: I don't believe in Santa.
CARLY: I don't believe in him either, not after the Santa Riots of Enkadar.
MOLLY: I am not even going to ask.

***

They ran down streets, past windows with twitching net curtains, towards a lane that only Carly could find. Every now and then, they would stop and catch their breath, but this also presented Molly with a chance to ask a few questions.

"Do you regret any of it?"

As questions go, this one was leading – but Molly had to ask it regardless.

"Of course I do!" Carly remonstrated sadly. "I deserve for people to hate me. They lost their children. I didn't help The Empress blow up the school, but I didn't stop her either. I tried in my own way, but it wasn't enough."

Molly didn't get a chance to say anything back.

A large shape stepped out from behind an equally large garden trellis.

But it wasn't The Endless Empress blocking their path.

It was Elvis.

"Is this actually for real?" Molly wheezed the cold out of her lungs.

Carly, however, looked absolutely petrified.

"In Enkadar," she reminded Molly, "you can be anything you want."

MOLLY: Is he one of Portia's loons?
CARLY: He used to be her therapist!
MOLLY: And he joined her in Enkadar and started dressing like Elvis?

***

Elvis grinned cheekily and pulled a crossbow out on the girls.

"Jesus, Joseph, and Mary!" Molly shrieked.

"Enkadar forever!" he yelled as a battle cry.

He fired a bolt, which swished through the air and embedded itself in a bush inches from Carly's forehead. She yelped in fright. Elvis didn't appear to be entirely familiar with the workings of a crossbow; he was toting it like a child with a nasty new toy. Carly threw herself behind a nearby car. Her old school instincts returned – the days when she took cover from airborne plates of chips and curry sauce.

A second bolt zipped through the air. It cut a hole in the car Carly had taken cover behind. She could smell the petrol tank bleeding onto the pavement.

"Call the police!" Carly yelled over to Molly.

And then she remembered why that would be a wasted call.

But Molly McCrumb wasn't going to surrender without a fight. "It's now or never," she muttered to Carly.

She rushed over and kicked Elvis in the crotch.

"Come on!" Carly gasped, seizing Molly's arm and pulling fast.

They were a few metres away when Elvis hollered:

"You won't be lonesome for much longer. Her Holiness is waiting for you."

Molly craned her head around in time to witness Elvis reloading his crossbow. His screeching fanatical laughter sounded nothing like the character he portrayed. He fired another bolt, but it went far off and slammed into a tree trunk.

"She is forever!" Elvis howled in the distance.

"What does that mean anyway?" Molly asked, jogging.

"It's something she used to say. She believes she'll rule Enkadar forever."

Molly thought that was rather pretentious of The Empress, but it suited her egotistical view of herself and the glorious state of Enkadar.

***

The X39 bus zoomed past Carly and Molly as they jogged by a row of grubby old houses. The auburn-haired woman behind the wheel tooted her horn and waved cheerily. The girls kept running, and Molly followed Carly's lead without question: so when Carly stopped – so too did Molly. And they stopped in the most run down area of Castlekrankie: a street infamous for damp old council homes, dumped immigrants, and high crime: Hillcroft Road. Worse than that, they came to a halt outside what had to be the dirtiest door of all the houses on the entire street.

Molly's thoughts, however, were with the X39 bus and the odd auburn-haired driver.

"That bus is never far away," Molly muttered. Something felt wrong.

Carly, however, wasn't listening to Molly.

"This place hasn't changed much," Carly said of Truman's home.

Molly McCrumb: Kickass Journalist waited as Carly knocked loudly on the door.

***

MOLLY: How will you destroy The Endless Empress?

CARLY: I have a deadly weapon!

MOLLY: Is it a gun or a knife or something else?

CARLY: Guns and knives always make a situation worse. No, this weapon is more practical than guns and knives. It is... [PAUSE] The Truth. I know a secret that can destroy a country.

MOLLY: [GASPS]

CARLY: The Empress is standing right behind me, isn't she?

PORTIA: Hello, darling. Come inside out of the cold... and bring the journalist.

HAMISH, THE SPYING HAMSTER

School was over for the day, but Enkadar and friendship were never over. With these things in mind, Portia decided to visit Carly. The Real World was bitterly cold, as usual. Truman didn't need to do any grocery shopping, so Portia was free to spend the day with her best friend. The dense skyline hinted at the coming of snow, which would replace the sleet. None of this bothered Portia: she liked snow, especially when it clogged up the roads, bringing delay and damage. A heavy blizzard was nature's favourite kind of anarchy.

Best of all, Portia thought as she skipped towards Carly's house, *heavy snowfall means all the buses will be cancelled.*

Buses did not exist in Enkadar. Buses were illegal in Enkadar. Her Holiness had declared it so!

Portia took a slight detour on her journey and stopped off at the local McDonalds. It was seething with litter. It was everywhere! Litter on the pavements, on the benches, in the shops, in the houses. It disgusted Portia. But she tried to block this out of her mind while she bought some Happy Meals. She'd already informed Carly that she wouldn't be having dinner at the Costello home.

No-one enjoyed a proper dinner at Carly's house.

Not even Carly.

***

"What *are* you eating tonight?" Portia asked Carly, her disgust blatant.

Carly didn't reply. For some reason, she suddenly felt an overwhelming urge to binge and purge privately. It seemed overly harsh, but she knew Portia was right to slate her eating habits. She wasn't the only one. But how could Carly tell her friends that she didn't know how to use a cooker or a microwave? She didn't know how to use them because…she didn't actually have a cooker or microwave in her kitchen.

The Costello kitchen contained nothing other than a television, table, sink and fridge. The place was bare, with yellow wallpaper from too many smoked cigarettes.

Carly did what she always did and faked enjoyment of her dodgy dinner.

"I'm making a crisp sandwich. Cheese and onion flavour. Mum bought really nice bread, and I just add a little butter to it. It tastes better than you'd think!"

Portia, upon realising that she had upset a fellow Citizen, smiled benignly and took Carly by the arm away from the table. She led her to a bag sitting on her kitchen counter: it held plenty of food for both of them.

"I always buy too much for myself," Portia lied, "so you might as well eat with me."

Carly grinned, touched at her friend's thoughtfulness. She didn't like the numbers inside the food, vile calories and saturated fats that would inflate her body shape.

Portia noticed Carly looking at the food with fear in her

eyes. She told her firmly:

"In Enkadar you can be anyone and anything you want! You are a princess, a legend, a beautiful role model with millions of fans."

Real life, Portia decided as she watched Carly eat, *is a parasite*. Real life required too much of the victim. Portia much preferred Enkadar. There was no corruption. No bad parents. No daft war memorials. No taxes. No buses. No litter. No churches.

There were, however, unicorns.

How could anyone choose the litter strewn streets of Castlekrankie over Enkadar?

But the litter Portia had in mind wasn't garbage. It was litter of the *human* variety.

Somewhere, in another country, a unicorn grinned and rainbows blossomed.

***

A few days later, Portia invited Carly over to *her* house. They shared a strange, frantic friendship, bonded by history and Enkadar. They were soul sisters. Portia had to demolish Carly's self-esteem every now and then, but she also elevated it too. It was her duty as a best friend, and as the Empress of Enkadar.

Carly had no idea what was about to happen when she arrived at the luxurious Pinkerton residence. Her new shoes were tight on her feet, and she was still trying to break them in even though she'd had them for nearly a year. Despite her nice black shoes, Carly felt slightly grubby; her clothes hadn't been washed for days because her mother wouldn't give her money for the launderette. This, Mrs Costello told Carly, was punishment for eating the last yogurt in the refrigerator.

The Pinkertons had money in the bank, and they weren't afraid to flaunt their wealth. It was something of a sore point for Portia. The image Portia had carefully cultivated was that of a bohemian artist-anarchist. It was completely at odds with her standing in the Real World. Carly marveled at Portia's enormous old house with the grand turrets, and she thought about Portia's fantasy: *Why do you prefer Enkadar to this grandeur?* she asked herself rebelliously. It wasn't a random question. She had in fact asked Portia that very thing before, but Portia seemed unsatisfied with everything – she always wanted something better, something of her own.

Carly took time to absorb her surroundings and found the brass lion attached to the door. It was clean, not a trace of rust. She raised the knocker between its teeth and slammed it down. She enjoyed the experience so much she did it again and again.

The door opened softly and Portia walked into the light.

"Follow me," she said with eyes twinkling in pleasure.

***

Portia escorted Carly into her kitchen. It was large and white with gleaming chrome fittings and glorious marble. Nothing was untouched by marble. The kitchen was a temple devoted to cookery! There were shelves crammed full of books, huge tomes with French titles that hinted at a sophisticated gastronomic experience.

Portia hugged her microwave; a large thing which could irradiate large portions.

"This is my microwave! You can use it any time you want."

Carly's grin reached her ears and she hugged the microwave too.

"And this is my oven!"

Portia kneeled before a rather hefty oven and pretended to worship it.

Carly laughed and joined in with the fun:

"You should get my mother to come here and see what an actual kitchen looks like!"

Portia shot that idea down instantly:

"She would probably think aliens have abducted her... she probably doesn't know what these strange devices do or how they operate."

The two friends laughed happily as friends often do when they're having fun.

Portia then showed Carly her pet hamster Hamish. He had been a Christmas present, and Portia showered the furry little thing with love and care.

Carly played with Hamish while Portia put the frying

pan onto the hot stove.

The ring was turned up to ONE, the lowest setting.

"Carly, darling" Portia said, as she cautiously retrieved Hamish from Carly's grip. "Could you please hand over the little unbeliever?"

Carly laughed again. This discussion was going in a peculiar direction, as often things did with The Endless Empress.

"We will not tolerate unbelievers!"

Portia dropped Hamish on the frying pan. Carly jumped up and cried out in horror.

"You're always in here listening to me! You think I don't notice?"

Carly could only watch as the hamster started jumping around the pan, trying desperately to save his little paws from the hot surface. She couldn't bear to watch Hamish endure pain. She had no idea why Portia had turned on him with such fury.

Portia continued her interrogation of Carly's hamster:

"What have you told your masters about Enkadar?"

Her hand turned the heat up until the dial reached FIVE.

"I see you do not want to talk!"

Hamish was leaping out of the frying pan for his life.

"STOP IT!" Carly screamed. "HE ISN'T A SPY! HE'S A HAMSTER!"

But Portia couldn't hear her, for she was trapped within the folds of fantasy.

"You're doing to him what was done to you on your eighth birthday," Carly wept.

This seemed to penetrate the dark parts of Portia's imagination. She savagely twisted the dial until it went to ZERO, and lifted Hamish away from the hot surface.

Then, unexpectedly, The Empress started stroking the terrified hamster:

"I'm sorry," she said as tears streaked her face, "I thought you were a spy from Milordahl, but you're just a cute little hamster, you wouldn't spy on me. Would you?"

***

Carly knew from that day onwards that her best friend – the girl she loved more than her own family – was beyond help.

And it was all Carly's fault.

SHE PUTS THE 'HIGH' INTO HIGH SCHOOL REUNION

The Hunt for the Endless Empress

As soon as Naima realised she was trapped within Truman Crapote's house, she rushed into his kitchen in search of a weapon. She had no intention of allowing Truman to do anything other than hold his baseball bat in a slightly menacing manner. But he didn't even try to pursue her. In fact he remained seated in the living room with his bat, nonchalantly rhyming off some words. As Naima moved out of the hall towards the kitchen, she distinctly heard the words THRILL and SPILL and HILL and KILL. A shiver fluttered through Naima: she didn't know if Truman's words (delivered in his slight voice) were the cause or whether her enforced withdrawal from gear was making her feel so weak.

In the past, Truman's home had been treated as a halfway house for the Citizens. He encouraged his friends to treat the place like it was their own. His mother didn't have any objections and she would drift away into her own private Enkadar. So Naima knew exactly where to go in order to find Truman's kitchen. She planned to seek out the cutlery drawer and give her old friend the same treatment she had given Kai.

The Empress would be blamed, of course.

Naima entered the kitchen – and found something quite extraordinary.

***

When is a kitchen not a kitchen? That was the question Naima asked herself as she explored. The usual centerpiece of a kitchen – that would be a refrigerator – looked completely incompatible with its surrounding. And yet this very kitchen reminded Naima of something else from the past. Why did it echo in her memory?

And then blissful clarity exploded out of her foggy gear-deprived head: Truman's kitchen looked like the pharmacy! But it had a slapdash quality about it. The room reeked like the chemistry classrooms at school, the same classrooms used to teach pupils about the periodic table and atoms and all that other stuff.

"Portia was always really good at chemistry," Naima said aloud.

But this wasn't just any old laboratory inside Truman's kitchen.

Naima's eyes widened as they took in the jars full of candy-coloured powders.

Each jar had a white label on it with neat words in LARGE print. The words on the jars proclaimed: DO

NOT INGEST IF ALLERGIC TO IMAGINATION. But even in her compromised state, Naima recognised the bright substance inside the jars.

Truman Crapote's kitchen was a gear lab.

Naima cheered in delight!

***

Naima suddenly became aware of another presence in the room. She remembered the reason for her detour into the kitchen. She hadn't yet found a weapon with which to defend herself! But it was already too late. Naima could hear *her* voice from the hall.

The Empress, flanked by Truman Crapote, walked into the kitchen with her hands behind her back. Naima looked her up and down, and then said:

"I can't believe you work as a waitress."

"It was a role," The Empress retorted. "But I can't remain in fantasy forever. There's nothing gratifying about that sort of life, darling. It was fun for a while, going undercover, pretending to be a citizen of Milordahl. But I always come back to Enkadar."

Naima had heard more than enough of this nonsense. She grabbed the nearest jar of gear (yellow!) and hurled it right at her old friends. Portia and Truman both dropped to the floor for protection as the jar shattered above their heads. Naima's surprise attack created a quick diversion – and mess all over the floor. But she wasn't fast enough!

On her way out, Truman blew Naima a kiss.

A thick cloud of gritty sparkling pink dust wafted from his hand.

It was pure undiluted gear, a dust of dreams.

And it hit Naima right between her eyes.

She inhaled the gritty cloud and staggered out into the hallway, caught in a haze of illusion. Her eyes and lungs full of powder, she frantically tried the front door handle, but it was still locked. She coughed and spluttered, but recovered swiftly.

"She's gone native!" The Empress cried out as she climbed to her feet. "I think we're too late, Truman. We can't rescue her from the Real World."

Truman laughed viciously, and said:

"Just so we're clear, I doused her in the newly enhanced batch of gear. She won't be in the Real World for a while, nowhere near!"

He stopped, and then did a crazy little dance in the mess of the kitchen.

"Do you think she'll see a dragon?"

"No," The Empress said, "but she might bump into your mum."

***

Naima was sitting at the top of the staircase, listening to vague voices floating up from downstairs. Her head felt light and frothy – but it wasn't a bad feeling. There was something familiar and comfortable in how she felt at that moment. Warm, fuzzy, nice, blanketed… free of damp flats and wailing brats. Then, without any prompting, a longing to explore the top level of Truman's home took hold of Naima. She suddenly had the desire to see how much of it had changed. Was it still the same as it had been back in high school, or was it unchanged like outside?

"Do I even want to know?" Naima asked herself in a booming voice.

***

"Did you kill the enemy agents?" Truman asked his Empress without rhyme.

"Every policeman in town is dead. And for good measure…I sent a sandwich hamper to the nearby army base. When war breaks out, we'll be unopposed."

The Empress stopped talking, but only so she could brush some sparkly yellow powder out of her hair. She felt disgusting. The stink of greasy cooking fat clung to her, making her feel grotty. It was completely unfitting for someone of royal blood to stink so badly. She needed a bath, but there wasn't any time!

"We should expect some old friends," The Empress said humourlessly.

That was the moment Carly and Molly chose to knock on the front door.

"Ah, they're here!"

The Empress glowed with expectation.

"Did you deliver the bombs to all the targets I selected?"

Truman nodded enthusiastically. The Empress smiled her satisfaction.

A new era was dawning for the world. And it would begin across a kitchen table.

HOW PORTIA PENELOPE PINKERTON LEARNED TO LOVE THE BOMB

No-one seems to remember who came up with the idea of a bomb. This constantly changes depending on whom I ask. Truman Crapote tells the story that Beehive Betty flippantly suggested it, and that the idea was later seized upon by the others. Naima swears blind it was Carly's idea. Carly claims Portia was the one behind it.

And Portia, of course, took full credit for everything.

"Guy Fawkes nearly blew up parliament with a bomb," Portia is meant to have said to the others.

It seems The Artist was inspired.

***

The remaining members of Enkadar's high council stood in the centre of the Embassy. There were no dragons, no unicorns, no rock stars, and no rainbows. Just four damaged teenagers, the last of the elite council.

It was the darkest day in the ancient history of Enkadar.

Beehive Betty and Captain Quirk had gone forever.

There was something else, something that would end in mass murder:

"I was taken into Mr Barton's office today," The Empress

started shakily.

Mr Barton was the esteemed headmaster of Castlekrankie High School. A fierce but dedicated old man, he was quietly concerned about the corrosive effect of Enkadar on the small group of pupils who comprised its Citizens.

"What did he say?" Truman asked.

The Empress trembled with absolute fury.

"I am no longer a student at Castlekrankie High. I've been expelled."

There was an angry uproar from the Citizens. How could he do this to Portia?

"He's an agent of Milordahl. He was clearly ordered to get rid of me."

"Why?"

"The authorities don't want people to know about Enkadar...they're afraid that once people know the Real World is a lie...they'll drop out and join me."

Then, quietly, with a crack in her voice:

"Mr Barton had the nerve to tell me that I have a history of bringing weapons into school. He reminded me of the time I pulled a gun out in Art class. He said the knife was one step too far."

But the situation was about to take a surreal turn. It was up to Naima to break the bad news. It had been relayed to her via text message.

This was going to go down about as well as a bucket of fish guts.

"The Hairspray Queen has formed her own independent nation. Captain Quirk hasn't decided whether he wants to join it or not. It's called Katraxa Prime."

The Endless Empress choked a little, because she couldn't form the words that spoke her turbulent emotions. She couldn't think of anything except what had happened in the playground, and all she could see was Captain Quirk clutching himself, trying to stem the flow of blood from his stomach.

"I didn't do it," she blurted. "It wasn't my fault."

"We know," Carly said softly, her voice disturbing nearby dust.

"This is unforgiveable," Truman cried out. "Betty's country is purely fictional!"

"That's what Betty said about Enkadar," Naima continued.

"What sort of a name is Katraxa Prime? It's terrible. It doesn't even sound like a real country!" The Empress said, with a childish stamp of her heel.

"That's what *everyone* says about Enkadar," Carly replied.

This drew a sharp glare from The Empress, who disliked having anyone tell her that Enkadar wasn't real. She could see clearly what was and what wasn't real.

"The situation is far worse than any of you think," The Empress admitted.

"Why?" Carly asked again. She felt curiously out of sync with her old friends.

"They know too much! Betty and The Captain were with us when we went after Darryl Meyer and got the wrong guy. They know about the Memorial. They're the supreme enemies of Enkadar. It's our word against their accusations."

Naima Supreme suddenly felt sick, and she leaned against Truman for support. Naima trusted Captain Quirk, but she had no idea what Betty would do. She was unpredictable, changeable, and her disloyalty had proved that beyond any doubt. Betty could destroy them all.

Naima imparted yet another shocking revelation:

"I overheard Captain Quirk telling Solara Jones he no longer believes in Enkadar."

The Empress gasped in disgust. After everything she had done for him! It was absolute treason. Worse, he was consorting with Solara Jones – the scummy gang member who had attacked her and Betty after school, the same witch Betty's sister Amanda had dragged around during their brawl.

Portia couldn't cope with such disrespect; it was an absolute affront to her sensibilities. This was an incitement to rebellion!

She wanted to crush the traitors into gory puddles.

But that eventuality had already been prepared.

"I have my suspicions about Betty and Quirk," The Empress spat. "I think they're spies for Milordahl."

The others stopped talking and looked at Her Holiness.

"It makes sense," she said urgently.

"They were our friends," Commander Carly countered in an uncertain voice.

"Friends do not betray friends!" The Empress bellowed. "They were spies from the Real World. It makes sense, doesn't it?"

Not to Carly it didn't. But she said nothing. She had allowed things to spiral away.

"Yes," Naima Supreme agreed.

"They're not allies, they're spies," Truman rhymed flippantly.

"Beehive Betty is going around telling people *she* invented Enkadar, and *you* stole it from her," Naima blurted.

It was all too much; the expulsion, the defection, the lack of respect shown to her exalted position. The Empress screamed and ranted and kicked walls and punched furniture. Everyone at school was laughing at her and Enkadar!

"We need to do something big," The Empress declared in an icy voice. "Bigger than holding up a mere classroom. We need to declare war on Milordahl."

She seemed calm, but Carly knew better. She could see in her eyes the same strangeness she had witnessed all those years ago after Portia's escape from the locker.

The Empress, always melodramatic, walked away from her subjects towards the wall at the far end of the Embassy. The wall, frequently covered in photographs of unbelievers, was now covered by a massive curtain held in place by heavy pins.

Carly wanted to know what was underneath the

grubby fabric.

She guessed it was two photographs: Betty and Captain Quirk.

But she was dead wrong.

Her Holiness pulled the sheet off the wall with a strangled scream.

Anything Carly might have said died there and then in her throat.

The wall was plastered with *hundreds* of photographs. For a moment, Carly thought it was a new style of wallpaper, but no, the photographs were pinned up one by one by one by one on the wall.

This latest plan hadn't just been decided upon, Carly knew that instinctively. It had taken weeks to get all of these photographs for the wall. This decision had been made long before Captain Quirk and Beehive Betty had left Enkadar, and before Mr Barton had expelled Portia.

"They're all people from Castlekrankie High School," Carly said, in case no-one else had come to the same realisation.

The Endless Empress shrugged her shoulders, and she repeated: "We need to do something big."

The Unicorn of Annihilation trotted into the room and aimed its bright horn at the wall. There was a tremendous flash of hot pink light – and the wall crumbled, letting in the light from beyond the Real World. Enkadar was ready for war!

The Empress felt better again.

But Carly Costello wasn't looking at the unicorn. All she could see were hundreds of faces looking down from the wall.

"All for one and death to all!" The Empress chanted.

"All for one and death to all!" Truman Crapote yelled.

"All for one and death to all!" Naima Supreme joined in, as her eyes fell upon photographs of the bitchy girls who had bad-mouthed her in the school toilets.

Commander Carly, however, remained silent.

***

How do you construct a bomb?

I'm not going to tell you, because that would be reckless. But making something out of nothing isn't as difficult as you may think. Common ingredients found in an ordinary household can be used to make an explosive device. If a person is inventive and wants to do it badly enough, they will find a way to create chaos out of calm. The Endless Empress did exactly that and she made a bomb. How? She reached into the Real World and found bits and pieces which, apart, made no sense...but which, together, made a weapon.

The Empress did something far worse than just *make* a bomb.

She used it.

CAKE POWER

The Hunt for the Endless Empress

Naima staggered around the upper level of Truman's council house, wandering from one experience to another; falling into other worlds, some of which vaguely recalled Enkadar. Naima had been on gear for years – it helped her escape the Real World. But what she was experiencing at that moment was a completely different height of insanity. Whatever changes Portia had made to the formula, it was unlike anything Naima had experienced. It was a hideous experience.

She found a door floating in front of her, so threw herself into it. The door gave way easily and Naima tumbled into a room full of dummies.

"Hello," she said with a hazy smile.

"Hello," the dummies chorused. "We live in the fantasy nation of Enkadar."

But there was something else in the corner…a chair with a woman sitting snugly on it, her large body wrapped in a patchwork shawl. An old-fashioned television played endless scenes of a soap opera. The woman's eyes were spacious but unfathomable. Naima found to her surprise that she recognised this pensioner.

"Mrs Stanza?" Naima ventured, her world clearing into reality for a second.

Mrs Stanza opened her mouth and spat out a fizzy

froth onto her lips.

Naima looked down towards the arm of the seat.

There was a plate with a large slice of cake on it.

Someone had baked Mrs Stanza a cake, except....

They had used white gear as a substitute for flour!

Why hadn't they used flour? Had it all been used up on something else?

A brief moment of clarity returned to Naima. She backed away with a scream.

Who would drug an innocent and defenseless person?

Actually, one dummy said in a cheery voice. *You do it all the time.*

***

Naima watched in fascination as more sparkling froth poured from the old woman's puckered lips. It was horrible, so she moved away slowly. Whilst moving back, Naima crashed into some of the dummies which served as Portia's constituents. Naima punched and kicked a few dummies, threatening to batter them if they touched her again.

Then her eyes fell upon the gun.

It was a rifle of some description. Long, thin and black.

Naima picked it up and decided to kill everyone in the house.

THE MASTERPIECE

There are two massive misconceptions about The Masterpiece.

Most people believe that there was only one bomb. In fact there were two. One was placed inside a lunchbox and delivered into the assembly hall. The other was taken into the canteen, next door to the assembly hall. Packed with flour – the main ingredient – and placed near the gas stoves...it leveled the entire school. Flour is flammable. It only takes a small spark to ignite it. And when the explosion occurred, it unleashed a dust cloud that burned away all the oxygen in the building. If any victims didn't burn to death in The Masterpiece, chances are they suffocated.

And what is the other major misconception about The Masterpiece?

Most people believe that The Endless Empress made her bombs without any help.

That is untrue.

She had the help of a loyal friend:

A boy with a knack for rewiring and writing truly awful poetry.

***

The Endless Empress arrived at school with the Sacred Lunchbox tucked tightly under her arm. She had spent over a week working and experimenting with her bomb. It had been a long but rewarding journey. The greatest scientists in Enkadar had helped craft the ultimate weapon; a powerful destructive mechanism that would obliterate the unbelievers. Truman helped too, and every now and then the Unicorn of Annihilation would arrive from Enkadar to help out.

"This is the end," The Empress said as pupils barged past her.

But it wouldn't be the end of The Empress.

***

The assembly was mandatory for all pupils at Castlekrankie High School. They were expected to attend with their teachers and listen as Mr Barton extolled the virtues of their school. He used the hour to boast, inform, educate and drum up some school spirit. And they had a lot to celebrate – because that deranged brat Portia Penelope Pinkerton had finally been expelled!

Teachers had actually toasted the news in the staff room with coffee.

***

The Hairspray Queen sat at the other side of the room

– and it was a big room – to Captain Quirk, who had decided not to participate in her foolish pestering of The Citizens. Betty stole glances at Quirk, who ignored her attention-seeking.

The Assembly Hall was crammed full of life and laughter.

Quirk looked around and found an entire world he didn't know existed. He had spent so long trapped in a fantasy; he had almost forgotten how to live a life. In a room full of people, Quirk felt utterly alone – but that wasn't bad. At least it was real. What he felt was valid… and it felt great, because it wasn't part of Enkadar.

Katy McGowan and Craig Keene sat in the row before him, tenderly holding hands, their public display of new love an exciting and glorious thing. Captain Quirk's heart pined for something as authentic as their new love.

Someone familiar moved past him through the swollen crowds.

Captain Quirk quickly realised that The Endless Empress had come to school.

But why had she brought lunch with her? he thought upon seeing her lunchbox, a tin container decorated with cartoon pony art. *She's expelled for what she did to me!*

A thin scar on the skin of his belly ached at the memory of being slashed in the playground. But Quirk quietly put the ache away; he was used to enduring pain. He refused to let either his father or The Empress win. Things were going to change.

But putting the ache away didn't answer the nagging question of why The Empress was at school.

Still, when Quirk looked around, he was thrilled to see Portia leaving the Hall.

And yet…she wasn't carrying her lunchbox.

***

Truman Crapote entered the school canteen without resistance.

The monitors and prefects, usually patrolling the corridors, were in the Assembly Hall along with the rest of the students. Everything else was eerily quiet. Truman never appreciated quiet, because he wasn't used to it. The only sound he could hear at that moment…was the sound of four little wheels squeaking on the smooth cafeteria floor.

Truman had spent the morning shopping for groceries, working his way down the list of special ingredients demanded by his Empress. He had found Planet Pound to be quite accommodating to his needs. Their famous Buy One Get Two Free offer was in full swing. So Truman had filled his trolley with every bag of flour on the shelf.

"Are you trying to break a world record?" the checkout woman had asked with a smile.

"No," Truman had smiled back, "I'm trying to bake a really big cake."

And now his trolley sat in the middle of Castlekrankie

High School's canteen, where the Citizens ate lunch, went to Enkadar and had chips thrown at them.

Truth be told, Truman felt rather guilty about stealing a trolley from Planet Pound. But after much soul-searching, he realised that in the grand scheme of things…it was a small price to pay for Enkadar.

He scanned the canteen, which was painted brown, and followed the gas pipes.

They led him to a cupboard, the wall of which faced the Assembly Hall.

Truman tipped the trolley over and got to work.

***

It didn't take long for the Citizens to get everything ready for detonation.

Her Holiness, Truman Crapote, and Naima Supreme met at a safe distance from their school. They stood on the snake bridge. It provided a great view so they could watch their work.

"Where is Commander Carly?" The Empress asked.

Truman and Naima looked at each other, but remained quiet.

"Where is she?" The Empress commanded yet again.

Naima finally came forward and said, "She has betrayed us, Holy One."

"No!" The Empress gasped. "She wouldn't abandon me again."

"Again?" Truman asked, not understanding what Portia was saying.

"Her recent contributions to our plan were subpar," Naima protested. "I don't think she wants to be part of Enkadar. Her heart isn't in it anymore."

A range of differing thoughts and feelings overwhelmed The Empress; hurt, confusion, and finally...anger.

"Then she can burn with everyone else," she hissed.

***

The morning announcements had already commenced when Captain Quirk felt his mobile phone vibrate in his pocket. He was thankful the sound was switched off. It was probably Portia or one of the Citizens. There was no way he intended to speak to any of them, so he sat quietly and listened to Mr Barton. The headmaster was talking about a rumoured amalgamation between Castlekrankie High and Bonnie Doon Academy. His voice, a low shaky thing, made him hard to understand.

Quirk suddenly realised Mr Barton looked terribly old and frail. His white hair was whiter than Quirk remembered. Maybe he would announce his retirement?

Quirk felt his pocket vibrate again, so he removed his phone as stealthily as possible.

It was Carly, desperate to reach him for some reason.

Quirk turned his phone off.

That's when everything went to hell.

A girl screamed from the back of the hall.

Then more people joined in with the screaming.

Quirk got up off of his chair to see what was happening,

And that's when he smelled something burning. It was a horrible fiery stench.

Panic and hysteria ensued as teenagers ran around aimlessly, frantically trying to find the source of the thick black smoke pouring out of the walls. Someone – a small pupil from first year – opened the cleaning cupboard. Teachers tried vainly to force their way to the back, but they couldn't get through the tide of terrified teenagers.

Captain Quirk tried to find Beehive Betty, but all he could see was the top of her wig hastily moving towards the emergency exit.

What the hell was going on?

A faint voice cried out,

"I think someone let off a firework!"

Sparks, pink and white, fizzed from a little tin lunchbox in the cupboard.

"There's flour in the cleaning cupboard!" The first-year pupil, whose name Quirk didn't know, sounded amused. Why would anyone put bags of flour next to cleaning products? It made no sense.

Then a deafening gust of fire exploded from the mouth of the cupboard.

The blast hit the young boy in the face.

He shot away and smashed into other teenagers.

Then, from the other side of the hall, there was a bigger

explosion.

Quirk screamed as dozens of people – boys and girls and teachers – somersaulted into the air. The smoke was thick and choking. Dust and powder floated everywhere in dark clouds. People were trying to escape through the windows and emergency exits.

But every single door and window had been locked or blocked.

Naima had made sure of it.

WE HAVE ALWAYS
LIVED IN ENKADAR
The Hunt for the Endless Empress

The Endless Empress led Carly and Molly down a dark hall towards the kitchen.

She stopped, spun around, and then threw up her arms with a triumphant flourish:

"Welcome to the glorious and wonderful world of Enkadar!"

Carly didn't bother trying to humour her old friend.

"I don't like what you've done with the place," she said tartly.

"I wouldn't worry about this old house," The Empress snapped back at her.

Then:

"It won't be here for much longer."

There was something in her words that iced Carly's blood, because she knew the Empress didn't deal in idle threats. She watched as The Empress leaned over and whispered something into Truman's ear. Her faithful Rottweiler-in-a-top-hat nodded lightly and walked past Carly and Molly, barely pausing to acknowledge his old friend as he said:

"You look great, Carly. You've put on a bit more weight. It suits you."

Carly shouted something incredibly foul back at him.

Truman stiffened, and walked away without saying a word.

Carly suddenly reacted with emergency speed.

"What did she tell him to do?"

Molly pulled a face, and then protested:

"How am I supposed to know? I don't have radar ears!"

Carly raised a quizzical eyebrow.

"You have a tape recorder. I'll distract the Empress, you check what's happened."

Molly McCrumb: Kickass Journalist sighed and slipped her hand inside her bag, brushing her fingers against the touch sensitive buttons. She rewound it quickly. Then she pressed PLAY. The volume was high, but the rucksack had muffled the sound. Nonetheless, she still heard the whispered exchanged between Portia and Truman.

***

PORTIA: Go downstairs and activate the timer for... say...twenty minutes.

TRUMAN: And then the bomb will sing a song?

PORTIA: Yessssss! Oh, it will sound so beautiful. The traitors will burn and their screams will mix with the music of the bomb.

***

Carly walked over to a nearby shelf, which looked

dangerously weighed down with glass jars full of powder. She lifted a jar and examined it carefully. It was crammed with gritty blue dust.

"Did you actually *invent* gear? Why?"

The Empress seemed delighted someone had finally figured it out.

"Yes I invented gear," she beamed proudly. "Some people lack imagination. Gear is a way of bringing them into Enkadar. It has proven very useful in getting new Citizens to join our army. We attract the losers, the disenfranchised and the college students." Then:

"Besides," she added, "it costs a lot of money to fund a country."

Truman returned to the kitchen, taking the jar out of Carly's hand.

"What the hell do you want with us?" Molly snapped, hoping to get this over and done with before the bomb downstairs went off. She was absolutely terrified.

"I want you to put this on," The Empress asked politely.

Molly had no idea where she got it, but it made her feel ferociously sick:

The Empress was holding a burned old beehive wig in her hands.

"I'm not wearing that damn thing!" Molly protested.

"WEAR IT OR I'LL SLIT YOUR THROAT!"

Molly reluctantly put the beehive wig on her head.

Beehive Betty stood in front of them – or a version of her at least.

"It's uncanny!" The Empress gasped. "You look exactly like her."

"How long have you known about it?" Molly McCrumb: Kickass Liar asked Carly.

"From the moment you walked into the café," Carly admitted contritely.

"You're Amanda McNab," The Empress stated, hoping to confirm her theory.

"Beehive Betty's older sister?" Truman asked, hoping to avoid being punched.

"Yes," Molly whispered. The wig on top of her head made her skin crawl.

"Now we're all here!" Truman said with a little clap of his hands.

***

But he was wrong.

Another guest was still due to arrive.

THE MAKING OF MOLLY MCCRUMB

Amanda McNab watched helplessly as the revolution was broadcast in slow motion. The end of her world arrived in the form of a crude bomb, and the apocalypse came complete with shaky mobile phone footage, flashing graphics, grave faces, concrete debris and human residue. Neat little captions were superimposed across the footage, while a bland voice casually informed the viewer: *This report contains images some viewers may find distressing.* But Amanda couldn't turn away because her sister's face was one of those shown on the *Six O'clock News.* The television transfixed Amanda into unconditional surrender.

Her parents, likewise, sat immobile in grief and disbelief.

Later on that night, as Amanda lay in her bed thinking about what had happened...she realised her parents hadn't once uttered Betty's name aloud since the news. That in itself was an unparalleled event in the history of the McNab household. Precious, perfect, perfidious little Betty was the chosen one: the daughter who got all the attention and love. The high standard Amanda couldn't match.

Not anymore!

***

We were Elizabeth and Amanda until we became Betty and Molly. No matter what we called ourselves, we remained the best of sisters and the greatest of enemies. We would bicker and attack each other but never allow others to do the same. It was okay for me to call Elizabeth names, but heaven help anyone else who did the same. It was true of Elizabeth too. She despised me for being her sister, and loved me for being her sister.

True sisterhood is a complicated and contrary thing.

I watched helplessly as the town recast my sister as a murderer in their tawdry little drama: *Guilt by Association*. But I knew Betty better than anyone. There was more to it. Something was rotten in the state of Enkadar, and I wanted to clean it up. Betty wasn't perfect, but she wasn't a murderer. I knew this because sisters know sisters.

University comes first and a job will come second, my father used to tell me long before The Masterpiece obliterated his other daughter. The Masterpiece changed him completely.

University no longer came first or even second. It didn't matter anymore.

You must make sure that monster pays for killing my Elizabeth.

A lot of parents sounded like that in the days

after the bomb.

Only revenge mattered and I wanted to become Dad's tool for that revenge.

One day I would return home and find Portia Penelope Pinkerton.

Then I would destroy her, just as she had destroyed my sister.

***

The news became a daily ritual for the family. It was Amanda's recovery, in a sense, because it made her realise what she wanted to do with the rest of her life. She wanted to find the truth; to patiently wait until the truth came to her. Amanda wanted to know the real truth, not the insane lies peddled by The Endless Empress – the same deceit that ensnared vulnerable people into her mad cult with pledges of salvation she could never deliver. Amanda had no boyfriend, she was twenty and had never been kissed – but none of that mattered to her. She studied hard and watched the news with her mother and father. That continued for a year until suddenly, one night, Amanda witnessed her father on live television.

He was waving a knife at the cameraman.

***

There had been a sighting of The Empress near the old industrial estate. There was nothing unusual in that, after all there were plenty of sightings of The Empress, usually in the most peculiar of places. No-one understood why Portia would return. The entire town wanted her dead! The witness – a bus driver – claimed she had watched The Empress ripping pages out of a James Patterson book near the abandoned plastics factory.

Someone at the police headquarters tipped off the newspapers and news broadcasters, and of course reporters from all around the country descended on Castlekrankie. A convention of cameras and microphones clogged the many roads and alleyways of the town.

Amanda's dad reacted differently when he learned why the press had arrived in town. He took a large knife from the cutlery drawer (the same drawer his wife arranged neatly on a daily basis) and followed the vans in his old Rover.

***

Amanda only found out her father had been arrested when she tuned into the *Six O'clock News*. He stood in front of the cameras waving a knife, calmly telling reporters he'd, "Come to see The Empress..." And that was all he got to say before being tackled to the ground by at least ten policemen.

It was a horrifying moment, the sort of memory that is

too strong to purge – that invades all thoughts and dreams. Amanda would never forget the day she watched her dad screaming for his dead daughter on live television.

Her mother's reaction, however, was quite startling and very different:

Mrs McNab stood up and calmly walked into the kitchen. Amanda waited.

Then it started. Amanda could do nothing other than watch as her mother calmly smashed every single plate in every single cupboard. They had more plates than Amanda had realised.

***

The horror of Betty's death had the same effect on the McNab household as it did on hundreds of others across the town: it froze families until they lived a parody of their former lives.

And The Empress got to live on as a fairy tale.

She simply vanished.

But what of the others involved in The Masterpiece?

Amanda attended the trial and watched from the public gallery…

***

The police van containing Carly Costello, Truman Stanza and Naima Calmar was on the verge of being tipped over by a furious mob. People screamed, yelled and spat globs of phlegm at the van. The teenagers were locked inside, protected from the ferocity of the crowd if not from the noise.

A group of policemen and policewomen in riot gear prevented the mob from breaking through the ranks. But everything went wrong when some of the police started attacking the van with their fists. Soon enough, there was an uprising.

The van moved gently around the corner of the courthouse and out of the reach of vengeful parents. But the Citizens of Enkadar could still hear what was being yelled:

"Where are the monsters who murdered my baby?"

"I'll kill them! I'll kill them! I swear I'll kill them! Please let me get them!"

"I hope you all burn in hell!"

The doors of the van opened and three teenagers climbed out of the back.

Truman was weeping inconsolably. He was dressed in a gorgeous suit of velvet. Even for his day in court, he couldn't help but overdress. Every now and then, he would melodramatically blow into a polka-dot handkerchief.

"It's an awful shame!" he wailed. "She left us to take the blame!"

The police in attendance said nothing. They didn't want to lose their jobs.

Naima Calmar was next to protest her innocence. She

did it in a remarkably calm manner. She seemed fully aware and in control of her situation. And, just like Truman, she was dressed in the latest fashions of Enkadar; a glossy green gown with matching flower pinned to her hair. It looked like a bloom had burst out of her skull. Inside she was utterly terrified – but when she spoke, she did so in a haughty voice.

"You can't prove a thing! The Empress planned and carried out everything. I was a victim of her manipulations. *She* should be the one in jail, not us."

Truman gave Naima a shifty side glance and smiled inwardly.

They had all agreed to put the full blame on Portia.

Carly Costello, dressed in a black suit loaned from her mother, remained absolutely silent. She was Portia's best friend, which meant the public hated her more than any other Citizen. Her eating disorder had worsened as a result of the stress.

***

The trial lasted eight hours before the jury reached a verdict:
The Citizens of Enkadar were found Not Guilty.

***

In other words:
They got away with it.

THE FINAL GUEST

The Hunt for the Endless Empress

Naima was finally ready to exact justice on the unbelievers.

The gun was heavy and she struggled to position it properly in her arms. The voices were getting louder and closer now.

"Murderer," she muttered under her breath.

Naima didn't know whether she was referring to herself or The Empress.

Then she leapt around the corner and aimed the gun at the startled visitors.

The Empress burst out laughing, which wasn't the reaction Naima had been expecting.

***

Molly McCrumb: Kickass Journalist stood by the kitchen door, sweating with panic; there was a bomb downstairs and it was going to explode in fifteen minutes. Nothing in Molly's life had prepared her for the level of terror she was experiencing in that house.

"We need to get out of here," she whispered at Carly.

"Have you forgotten about the advert in the Castlekrankie Chronicle?"

Molly hadn't forgotten about it, but she couldn't take

much more tension. She wanted revenge, but she also wanted to keep her body and sanity intact. She couldn't take any more unwanted surprises.

Naima leapt out from behind the door, cursing and swearing, a lunatic on the run.

She swung around and aimed something at The Endless Empress.

"It's loaded," Naima croaked.

Carly covered her mouth at the sight of Naima. She couldn't believe the girl in front of her was the same girl she'd been friends with during high school. The fresh-faced beauty – whose exotic looks had made her the envy of girls in every class – had gone. In her place was a haggard waif in a tracksuit. She looked completely at odds with the refined girl they had known before everyone had turned on her.

"I'm going to shoot you all and save the world from invasion by Enkadar."

Molly didn't know how to respond to Naima's mad statement.

"What have you done to her?" Carly snapped at The Empress.

"Truman doused her in super gear! It's a new twist on the classic formula."

"Gear is a vile blight on society," Molly snapped angrily.

Naima, ignoring this exchange, aimed the rifle at Portia – and pulled the trigger.

***

Nothing happened.

Naima closed her tired eyes and when she opened them again, the rifle in her hands was no longer a rifle. The Empress cracked up with vindictive laughter.

"Did you seriously intend to shoot me with a broom?"

Naima dropped the broom and clutched at her forehead.

"I thought...I thought it was a gun...but that's impossible..."

"Thirteen minutes," Molly piped up.

Commander Carly smiled at her old friend:

"It's good to see you again, Naima."

But Naima's gear-corrupted eyes were now fixed firmly upon Molly McCrumb.

"You look like The Hairspray Queen," she said unkindly.

"I'm her older sister," Molly replied smoothly, ignoring Naima's hostile tone. "And if you speak to me like that again, I'll punch you out the door."

"You're much prettier than Betty," Naima said snippily.

Carly decided to cut through all the background noise with a question:

"Why did you announce a reunion in the local newspaper?"

But Portia's reply was so unexpected that it took Carly's breath away.

"I didn't place that advert in the newspaper, darling."

"But if you didn't…who did?"

Molly wasn't thinking about the advert, she had other things on her mind.

"Twelve minutes," she said to herself.

***

Truman Crapote left the kitchen to check the door. He wanted to make sure his escape route was ready for a sharp exit. When he reached the front door, he stopped and considered his mother. He didn't want to kill her, but she was so old and infirm. The Empress believed in euthanasia, in assisted dying. Portia had assisted *many* people in dying – all of whom hadn't actually wanted to die, but that was irrelevant.

The Empress assured Truman that her special cake would be a sweet deadly pill.

"Your mum will slip into Enkadar…and then go to Heaven."

Besides, all the flour was needed for the bomb downstairs.

With that in mind, Truman decided to go and check the thermal detonator.

He was about to slip downstairs when something caught his eye.

Through the dirty glass on his front door, Truman saw a big red bus move slowly down the street and come to a halt outside his house.

"The X39 is parked outside. Is it our escape ride?"

The Empress heard him from the kitchen.

"I didn't order a bus! I loathe buses. I have an ice-cream van in the garage."

Truman nodded agreeably, because his Empress spoke only the gospel truth. He peered through the glass and watched outside for signs of activity.

He saw the bus doors open and heard their hiss. Then a shadow moved out and swiftly crossed the street towards Truman's house. It didn't look like anyone he recognised. He waited for whoever it was to knock at the door.

The shadow paused at the door. Truman waited, his breath caught in his chest. The shadow then did knock on the door, but they didn't use their hand. Instead, they used an axe. Truman knew it was an axe because he could see its blade through the gash.

Truman yelled as the second knock caught the edge beside the lock and sent his front door crashing into him.

The world spun and he fell onto the floor, pinned down by the entrance/exit to his home.

A large boot stamped his face into oblivion.

***

The noise from the hall brought everyone running to see what had caused it.

Someone crossed the threshold and into the house.

"You'd better have a good explanation for barging

in here!" The Empress screeched. "This is the official Embassy of Enkadar. You are not welcome here!"

A middle-aged woman with auburn hair, clutching a rather large axe, gave Portia a truly filthy look. She wore a uniform. It was dirty and wrinkled.

Molly recognised her immediately.

It was the driver of the X39 bus.

"Why are *you* here?" Molly asked in her journalist voice.

"I've come to kill you all," the bus driver said calmly, brandishing her large red axe.

The others backed away into the kitchen and prepared themselves for a fight not all of them would survive.

'FOREVER' IS A SMALL WORD WITH A BIG MEANING?

The Hunt for the Endless Empress

It explained quite a lot of things that made no sense: The X39 always seemed to appear at odd moments, driving down roads that were far from its actual route. Carly had noticed the X39 during her travels. The Empress had also observed it, as she observed all buses. Naima had encountered the X39 too. But none of them had thought anything of it – because no-one pays any particular attention to a bus. Buses are everywhere. They blend into the world. They're around us day and night. We use them and forget about them.

The X39 was the perfect cover for someone wishing to spy on the Citizens of Enkadar.

***

"Do you know who I am?" the bus driver asked the little crowd.

"No," The Empress stated. She was impatient to oversee the war effort.

"Reunion, reunion, high school reunion..." Naima said fuzzily.

But the bus driver didn't hear or care about Naima. Instead, she turned her gaze on Carly. There was an unspoken connection, something they knew about each other.

Carly understood instantly what this woman represented.

"You've been sending me letters. You're my Conscience, aren't you?"

"YES!" she mocked. "Why didn't you kill The Empress?"

"I'm not a murderer," Carly said quietly. "I'm sorry, but you have me wrong."

The bus driver, unsatisfied with Carly's response, raised her axe and swung it at the nearest wall, which held dusty portraits of Truman as a baby. (He'd been a bratty baby.) The others – with the exception of The Empress – jumped away twitchily as the axe smashed into the hard surface. Then the driver trailed it behind her, the butt end dragging noisily along the laminate flooring.

Molly's fear suddenly turned into seething anger. The bomb downstairs would detonate in less than ten minutes. She had to get the hell out of this nightmare!

"I don't deserve to be lumped in with these people," Molly cried out incredulously. "I'm here to get revenge on The Empress as well."

The driver fixed her wet eyes on Molly, thick auburn hair falling over her face.

She had found a potential new ally:

"Why take revenge on The Empress when the others

were involved? Kill them all! There's a killer here! KILL HER!"

To punctuate her point, the bus driver slammed her foot down on the door that pinned an unconscious Truman Crapote beneath it. He didn't cry out. He couldn't.

"Who are you anyway? Do you work for the authorities of Milordahl?"

The bus driver finally confessed her interest in the Citizens:

"Do you remember my daughter, Laura Daniels?"

The Citizens of Enkadar – Portia, Carly, and Naima – looked at each other.

"I've never heard of her in my life," The Empress shrugged.

"Did I sit next to her in History?" Carly asked, racking her brain for a face.

"She didn't take History!" The bus driver dangled the axe dangerously.

Naima, still under the power of gear, muttered something about cake.

***

The bus driver had spent years planning ways to hurt the Citizens, just as they had hurt her by murdering her daughter during The Masterpiece. She wanted to run over them in her big red bus. But that wasn't good enough. She wanted to kill them so many times over that it hurt her internal organs.

Putting the advert in the Castlekrankie Chronicle had been her way of letting them know she was coming to get them. The bus driver would follow them until they led her to The Empress, and then she would get them together.

All in loving memory of her beautiful daughter, Laura.

Laura, with her auburn hair and freckles, was *everything* until The Masterpiece.

So it was with some surprise that the Citizens couldn't actually remember Laura.

Laura was just one in one thousand victims; another face in the school yearbook.

And for Laura's mother, a bus driver…this was the ultimate insult.

***

Then the Empress did something to completely tip Laura's mother over the edge, as though she hadn't toppled over it already. Even Carly couldn't believe Portia's timing.

What did she do to upset the psychopathic bus driver?

The Endless Empress yawned.

The bus driver screamed a painful scream.

"Eight minutes," Molly yelled over her howls.

But another, more urgent sound took over.

The ground rumbled noisily, and then it cracked beneath Molly's feet.

Suddenly, horrifyingly, the floor exploded outwards.

Wood chip and concrete shrapnel shot out and shattered glass jars and smashed windows. Heat – horrible heat – scorched up from an inferno below the ground.

The house grumbled and fire burst out of the floorboards.

"My dragons have come to save me!" The Empress declared, thanking the fire.

Then the explosive shockwave from the bomb downstairs hit everyone upstairs.

***

Yes, Truman had bungled the timer.

WAR

The Hunt for the Endless Empress

I came to take revenge on The Empress. I
wanted justice for my sister.

Dying wasn't part of my plan.

***

Minutes passed slowly until Molly opened her eyes. They
were caked in dirt, soot, and brightly-coloured powders
from cracked jars.

Gear!

Molly pressed her hands onto the kitchen floor and
pushed herself upright. If the flames didn't kill her, then
overdosing on gear might. She *had* to get outside.

The world around Molly was utterly destroyed, a
miniature version of The Masterpiece. The shelves with
heavy jars were mostly wrecked, although some still
remained intact. Molly surveyed the wreckage and found
Carly was still alive, albeit unconscious. The Empress was
stirring and the bus driver lay close by, in the hall.

There was no sign of Naima.

Truman was probably dead, because where his door
had pinned him there was now a huge gaping hole in the
ground. Molly screamed in fear, because she could see
the basement beneath and feel the thick heat of the fire

burning through it.

Then, suddenly, a murderous notion took over Molly.

She could kill The Empress and blame it on the fire.

It would be so easy. The bus driver might even be held responsible.

Molly had spent so long looking at photographs of The Citizens, researching their lives, thinking their thoughts, dreaming their dreams...that she had nearly become them. She wanted to avenge her sister, and had lied in order to get close to her sister's friends. Her desire to kill Portia was strong.

But Molly knew deep down she couldn't stoop to that level.

I won't do it. I don't want to live in Enkadar.

Molly darted over to where Carly lay and slapped her face hard.

"Get up!"

"It's too late," a voice said from behind Molly.

She slowly turned, to see The Endless Empress rising to her feet.

"We're going to flood the streets of Castlekrankie with gear...and soon everyone will be in Enkadar...and more bombs will go off...and the Real World will surrender! We will win the war against Milordahl, or die trying!"

The sound of Portia ranting was enough to waken Carly from her coma. She was up and running towards the gaping wound where the front door had previously stood.

But so too was the bus driver.

The driver and The Empress turned on each other.

The Empress lifted a jar of green gear from the remaining shelf.

The bus driver moved to lift her axe.

But the axe handle was roasting hot; a result of sitting in the flames.

The bus driver screamed and fell away. Her hand sizzled noisily.

The Endless Empress raised her jar and brought it down on the driver's skull.

Something cracked...but it wasn't the heavy glass jar.

The bus driver – Carly's Conscience – toppled over and dropped though the hole, into the basement.

A hot gush of pink fire shot upwards and then faded into smoke.

The Empress wrapped herself in the tattered remains of Enkadar's flag.

Then she turned and faced Carly and Molly.

"You damn war criminals! I'm going to execute both of you bitches!"

She flashed a gleaming razor blade from beneath the folds of her flag cape.

"But it's time for me to make a...sharp...exit."

***

Carly pressed her back against the wall in the hallway,

just opposite the collapsed staircase by the kitchen. She moved around the gaping hole, and slowly inched herself towards the outside world. Molly, mindful of what had happened to Truman and the bus driver, copied her exact moves, step by step, inch by inch.

The Empress lunged and slashed at Molly's rucksack.

"I'm going to get you like I got your vicious kook of a sister!"

Molly squealed, not only because of the insult, but also because her precious Dictaphone was inside her bag:

"I'll punch you in the face if you try that again, you loony!"

The Empress grabbed Molly's bag with one hand, and slashed with the other. "You were supposed to die in the fire!"

Molly pulled the rucksack away from Portia with all her strength.

The Empress nearly fell sideways into the fire, but she regained her balance…

And followed the two girls outside into the Real World.

***

They managed to escape Truman's house, and the fiery carnage within.

The street was full of people, some dressed in pyjamas. Some were neighbours who would rather watch the drama in front of them than a soap opera on TV. Others had fled their homes to escape the spreading fire. But everyone kept a safe distance from the girls. One or two of them even phoned the police, which didn't make the slightest difference.

No help would come from the outside. The Endless Empress had made sure of it.

"Where can you run to anyway?" The Empress demanded. "I know high people in low places. They won't stop until you've been exterminated."

"She's lying," Carly said. "It's just another of her fantasies."

"I make my dreams come true," The Empress stated with a swish of her razor.

"She thinks she's at war with us," Molly announced to everyone.

The neighbours stood passively, filming everything on their mobile phones.

"You're all useless pigs," The Empress hissed with wide moon eyes.

*Wide **loon** eyes*, Molly thought creatively.

"I've sent out special packages to selected targets. I've sent bombs to the butcher, the baker, the candlestick maker. And I didn't forget the hospital, the airport, and the power stations. The bombs will continue until Milordahl surrenders to Enkadar."

***

Molly suddenly remembered back to her meeting with Truman, earlier that day whilst she was interviewing Carly in Go Joe's Café. He had been laden with shopping bags, all full of groceries. And he had told her he was heading to the post office.

"He delivered the bombs this afternoon!" Molly gasped in sudden understanding.

And that meant it was already too late to stop them reaching their targets.

***

Carly shouted something at Portia, but the sound of Truman's house exploding stopped Molly hearing it exactly. Molly's ears popped and a painful ringing invaded them. There was a shouted conversation going on right in front of her. And whatever Carly had said – the effect was dramatic.

The Endless Empress looked as though her world had suddenly ended.

The ringing in Molly's ears slowly faded out.

"No…" she heard Portia gasp. "No!"

"It's true," Carly admitted sadly.

Ah, thought Molly, *this must be The Truth…her secret that can destroy a country.*

But what did she say?

The Empress burst into tears and flung herself at Carly. From the side of her tired eyes, Molly could see someone approaching rapidly down the road.

She turned and backed away in astonishment.

Naima had escaped Truman's house, but she was still in Enkadar.

And she had taken the bus driver's keys.

"You ruined everything!" The Empress yelled as she throttled Carly.

Carly, with all her strength, pushed Portia away from her…

The Empress fell onto the road.

"I AM FOREVER!"

The X39 bus smashed into The Endless Empress, dragging her down the street until Naima figured out how to put her foot down on the breaks.

It took her a while.

Molly watched in horror as the bus came to a grinding halt.

Naima stumbled out of the sliding doors.

"I didn't kill her," she wept, "it was The Endless Empress. She killed her!"

"That *was* The Endless Empress!" Naima pointed out.

The Endless Empress wasn't forever after all.

SECRET OF ENKADAR
The Hunt Is Over

The Endless Empress didn't die.

Portia Penelope Pinkerton existed in a hospital bed, with wires and tubes around and inside her body. Her brain had been traumatised as a result of Naima's bad driving, but technology kept her alive and well-fed. Her eyes hadn't opened once since her arrival at the hospital. She was under protective custody, not only to protect her from the mob on the street outside, but to protect the doctors and nurses in case she awoke.

But the consensus was that Portia Penelope Pinkerton would never wake up.

Five people had already tried to turn her machine off.

Three of them were nurses.

But Portia had no intention of returning anyway...

***

The great shining city of Nacka was suffused in the rays of perpetual sunshine, everlasting, just like The Endless Empress of Enkadar. Portia sat on her golden throne, looking down on her people. They all loved her. Portia couldn't even go out for a curry without people screaming her name.

This was true paradise. Enkadar was real. Portia was

elated to finally be in Enkadar without any distractions…
and she had found salvation beneath the wheels of a bus.
A damn bus! She knew that somewhere else, somewhere
in The Real World of Milordahl, she was strapped to a bed,
kept alive by machines and human rights campaigners.
But it didn't matter. She looked over at the Unicorn of
Annihilation and nodded her head regally. The Unicorn's
horn glowed brightly.

"Are you enjoying your parade?" The Unicorn asked.

"Yes. I want one every single day!"

There were floats moving down the golden streets
towards the palace. Massive balloons blotted out the
skyline, all different shapes and colours and sizes. The
people cheered deafeningly as the floats moved past
them.

"I have what I've always wanted," The Endless Empress
said to a roaring crowd.

She was truly free of the Real World.

And it felt great.

But The Unicorn had an unexpected surprise for his
Empress. The parade was coming to an end when The
Empress looked down at the final float to see…

A gigantic red bus full of people she immediately
recognised.

"No!" The Empress shrieked. It wasn't possible!

The bus had brought all the victims of The Masterpiece
to Enkadar.

***

Even though The Empress was immune to the effects of gear, she had conveniently forgotten to immunize Truman Crapote. He survived the fire, but with horrible burns. His mind was as addled by long-term exposure to The Empress as it was by gear.

The bus driver had an actual name too. She was Noreen Daniels, and before she followed the Citizens around in her X39...she drove the school bus. Not only did she lose her daughter, she lost all of the teenagers she drove each day.

But Noreen's wasn't the only body in that house. The paramedics also found old Mrs Stanza upstairs on her chair, another victim of the madness unleashed by The Empress.

To this day, no-one knows if Portia meant to kill Truman's mother.

And what happened to the bombs? Most of them were recovered, but the newly privatized postal service was a bit too efficient: some bombs reached their targets. Eighteen packages have since gone off, but three remain unaccounted for – and the bomb disposal squad is on high alert. No-one knows if or when the remaining bombs will go boom.

***

Soon after finishing the initial draft of her report, Molly McCrumb decided to pay Naima Calmar – formerly Naima Supreme – a visit. The prison was falling to bits – although it was still cleaner than Go Joe's Café – and the security guards enjoyed frisking Molly, a little bit too much. But Naima looked *amazing* in the flesh. Molly almost didn't recognise the girl behind the glass. Gone was the addict who had run over The Empress whilst off her face on gear. In her place was a clean, intelligent, alert person. She spoke clearly and concisely. Her eyes blazed with light.

This was the girl Naima should have been all along.

"Hello," Molly said as Naima smiled lightly.

"I'm glad you came to see me," Naima said.

"You look great!" Molly blurted out.

"I feel great too. In a strange sort of way…coming here has been one of the best things in my life. I'm in protective custody, obviously. But I'm clean. I'm on track. I'm even seeing my daughter this weekend."

Molly heard something in Naima's voice that wasn't there previously.

"You miss her, don't you?"

Naima nodded. She seemed overwhelmed with emotion, but pushed it aside to concentrate on the reason she had summoned Molly. "I've been an idiot, Molly. But I'm going to make everything work for me. I'm not living in the past anymore. I'm going to get out of here and raise my daughter alone. We don't need anyone else."

Then:

"Have you finished your report?"

Molly grinned:

"It's no longer a report. It's going to be a book. I want to call it *Dead Teenagers*, but my publisher is a bit reluctant."

"I'm glad you're getting it out there, but does it have the proper ending?"

Naima didn't seem to want to say anything more, but there was something in her manner that suggested there was more to say. Something Molly hadn't cottoned onto yet; a missing part of the puzzle.

Naima didn't let Molly go away completely empty handed.

She gave her this,

"Whatever Carly told you about the day Portia met The Bookworm is a lie."

***

I had to go through the tape again, because it had recorded everything from that night. Naima's words made me realise that there was still something missing from my story; I had overlooked something obvious. Carly had told me she had a 'secret with the power to destroy The Empress' – but she didn't give me any other details. She didn't get the chance. It was only by revisiting the tape that I discovered the secret. It wasn't easy. I had to have the recording enhanced. I had to improve the clarity of sound until the whisper became loud enough to hear.

But I finally heard a furtive exchange between Carly and Portia in the kitchen, words I did not hear at the time. It confirmed what Naima had told me. It gave a genuine reason for Carly's guilt over The Masterpiece. It told me why Carly went mad with grief. And for the first time ever, I felt genuine sympathy for Portia. I never thought I could feel anything but hate for her.

But my recording explained everything.

It revealed The Truth; the secret behind Enkadar; the core that turned an entire world, until it spun madly out of control.

And not even Naima knew the full extent of Carly's involvement in Enkadar.

***

CARLY: I saw him that day. I could have warned you to run.

PORTIA: What?

CARLY: I saw The Bookworm watching us at the factory. But I said nothing.

PORTIA: Shut up! Shut up! Shut up!

CARLY: I let him get you because I was angry at how you treated me.

PORTIA: I was inside that locker for days…

CARLY: What happened to you was my fault. I'm genuinely sorry.

(SILENCE)

CARLY: I brought the knife to school.

PORTIA: *You* ruined everything!

***

The email arrived in my Inbox a few weeks after my meeting with Naima. I knew it was from Carly even before I opened it, because the subject line was written in CAPS, and it had been sent during the early hours of the morning. Only one person stays up that late, and up until the moment I read the email…I never questioned why Carly couldn't sleep.

The email was titled:

THE TRUTH

I opened Carly's email and she told me the rest of her story:

***

I wasn't completely honest. You'll know that by now. You've got everything on tape, so you can tell the story the way it should be told. I blame myself for what happened to Portia. The Bookworm could have taken me too, but I gave him Portia. That was my birthday present to her. My best friend! I stayed with her for years. Sometimes, when I was brave enough, I stood up to her. I saw the effect she had on people. My own life was so bad that for a while…even Enkadar was better. Then one day, I decided to stop her. I took a knife into school. I wanted Portia to be caught with it. I wanted Mr Barton to ban her from school forever. I didn't mean for Quirk to be hurt in the fight.

My plan worked, but it made everything worse. Your sister was nasty and manipulative.

She has nothing on me though.

I'm scared, Molly. I'm so scared. Someone is following me. He thinks I don't know, but I see him peering through my window at night. AND I LIVE ON THE FIFTH FLOOR! When I told you there were other Citizens of Enkadar, it wasn't a lie. Elvis…well, Dr Isosceles, hasn't been caught. And there are other cranks too. They could be anywhere. They could be your postman, your neighbour or the door-to-door salesman. The Empress might be in a coma, but her followers are everywhere.

They'll come after both of us. Don't trust anyone. Don't accept parcels from people you don't know. And never eat the sandwiches!

Yours sincerely,
Carly Costello

***

Molly didn't know what to make of the email, but it was clear Carly was living in fear. She was used to living in fear, of course, but this was a different kind of fear. Molly sat in front of the screen without any idea of what to do next. She considered replying to Carly, but had a sense of foreboding. That Molly would never see Carly again was a certainty, but she also had an instinct the story wasn't over. There was another paragraph to write, an epilogue to insert.

But what was going to happen next?

***

A sudden noisy interlude broke Molly's quiet deliberation.

Someone was outside her front door, jabbing at the rarely used door bell.

"It's the postman," a deep voice called from behind the door.

But Molly knew it wasn't the postman, for he had

already delivered the morning mail.

The doorbell rang again, and again, and again in a loop. It was being pressed in a frenzy. The ordinary sound of the doorbell suddenly became a terrifying thing.

"Open the door," the postman hollered through the letterbox,

"I have a special delivery for you, little pig."

THE END